Tropic Lights

Tropic Lights

Gerald Lebonati

Knights Press

Stamford, Connecticut

Designed by Able Reproductions, Copyright © 1985
Cover designed from an idea by the author

Published by Knights Press, P.O. Box 454, Pound Ridge, NY 10576

"Only In Miami" © 1982 Warner-Tamerlane Publishing Corp & Too Tall Tunes. All Rights Reserved. Used by Permission

Library of Congress Cataloging in Publication Data

Lebonati, Gerald.
    Tropic lights.

    I. Title.
PS3562.E264T7   1984   813'.54   84-19414
ISBN 0-915175-05-3 (pbk.)

Printed in the United States of America

1.

They were good for one another. John was tall, broad-shouldered, attractive, though not in a pretty sort of way. His eyes were brown, lighter toward the center, and deep-set. His short, thick hair was combed straight back. His black jacket tapered at the waist to reveal the narrowing of his torso and a bow tie was knotted tightly around his neck.

She was like a picture out of a magazine, all touched up and perfect. Her skin stretched smoothly over an angular jaw; her cheekbones were high and sculptured, while a mass of long dark hair fell down behind her ears, pierced with glittering stones. Her soft hazel eyes glowed richly against her sun-darkened complexion. She never considered modeling because she hated the idea of using sex to sell cameras and chewing gum.

John escorted her down the red-carpeted stairs. They looked very natural together—the perfect couple. Little old ladies would see them and sigh.

The Theatre of the Performing Arts was filled to capacity that evening. The ballet was captivating. So was the audience. During the intermission they sipped champagne together and watched the parade of faces. After the performance they moved with the rest of the crowd to the lobby, following the exit signs toward the tall glass doors. Caught in the middle of the large crowd, they could barely move. Once they passed through the doors, however, they were free. The South

Florida breeze tousled Janet's hair, causing her thin black gown to cling revealingly to her slender body. Once again John noticed how delicately proportioned she was. The jacket of his tuxedo flapped in the spring breeze as he guided her toward the parking lot. The moonlight illuminated the top of the stately Royal Palms. Their fronds shone green in the thick blue night.

John had met Janet at the office six years ago, and they seemed to get along from the start. They shared a space on the north side of the huge room that was sectioned off by brightly colored partitions. Every morning at 8:05, they huddled together over a coffee cup, sharing the adventures of the previous night. One of the guys on the opposite side of one of the partitions used to peer over and make loud comments. This lack of privacy increased the vague uneasiness John had whenever he talked about his experiences. They usually sounded so ambiguous and brief. Nevertheless, John felt that he and Janet were getting closer and closer as friends, yet, at the same time, he also perceived a door between them that he was afraid to open. Sooner or later he would have to make that uncomfortable move to really reveal himself. The anticipation grew stronger day by day. When he finally worked up the courage to tell her that he was gay, he had given the disclosure such a buildup that when he got to it, her reaction was an expectant, "go on." And when he said, "that was it," the moment was anti-climactic, almost as if she were disappointed that his news wasn't more dramatic. For his part John thought it was dramatic enough, but Janet didn't seem to care about his sexual preferences. They were friends, not lovers. Why did he even go through the bother of hiding it, reversing pronouns, and speaking in ambiguities? It was all so draining. The whole thing was amusing in retrospect, although at the time it had been undeniably difficult. Since then they had gone on to different things; John had left to study art in the South of France, and Janet had moved to a new and better job. Yet time had not eroded their friendship. Here they were, back in the same city, working for the same company once again, and still talking to one another.

John tucked her into the passenger seat of his aerodynamically correct sports car and dashed over to the other side. "Well, what do you think?" he asked as he got into the driver's seat. "Should we go to the party in the Grove or not?"

"Sure, why not?" she said.

"I don't know how many men there'll be for you," he warned.

"Oh, I don't care. Let's go."

"You sure?"

She widened her eyes and nodded. John hoped that it would be a mixed group for her sake. The car sped along the McArthur Causeway which connected Miami Beach to the mainland. Water lapped up to the raised highway on either side, as it stretched from island to island over the bay. Giant white cruise ships, strung with lights from fore to aft, sat motionless next to green and white striped canopied ramps. As the road curved, the tall gleaming buildings of downtown Miami swung into view, their lights reflected in the still waters. Then the expressway rose steeply, banked to the south, passing the flashy high-rise condominiums of Brickell, before it sloped down again into the overgrown brush of Coconut Grove. John turned left onto LeJeune Road, which separated Coconut Grove from Coral Gables, and then made another left onto Kumquat Avenue. As they penetrated deeper into the Grove, they passed under vaults of tropical Poinciana and Ficus. Coconut Grove was the thorn in Ma Bell's side. Trees sprang up everywhere, regardless of telephone wires. It was the African Jungle, with paved streets and boutiques. It was camping out with dinner at Café Europa.

They drove up to a large house hidden in the vines and shrubs. Its rough-hewn, wooden front seemed to grow out of the natural landscape. Cars were scattered about the area as if some giant hand had randomly thrown them about. John pulled the brake and hoped that no one would park behind him. "Here we are, beautiful." He got out and opened the door for his friend.

"God, these things are low," Janet said, as she struggled to get out of the car. He came around and supported her, as her high heels sank into the soft earth. She tiptoed to the walkway, a series of round stepping stones that lead up to the porch. The house was pulsating to the sound of Gloria Gaynor belting out the last strains of "I Am What I Am." They went up three steps and John pushed the lighted button next to the name WILSON. Finally, on the third ring the door flew open.

"Hi," said the stranger on the other side.

"Hi, I'm a friend of Charles' and this is Janet."

"Come on in. My name's Ralph. Make yourself at home. The booze is over there," he pointed somewhere to his left. "There's food on the table, and Charles was here a minute ago. He'll be right back."

"Thank you." As they walked in, everybody turned to see who had arrived. John was embarrassed, though Janet had said that he looked terrific in his black tuxedo. And she was definitely a knockout in her slinky, low-cut dress. The only thing wrong was that everyone else was in jeans and tee-shirts. He turned to Janet, who was smiling.

"You're enjoying this, aren't you?" he said.

"Of course. Why shouldn't I?"

"You could at least show a little discomfort."

"I think you're doing a good enough job for the both of us. Relax. Enjoy yourself. Come on." She grabbed his hand. "Let's get a drink."

"Lead the way." She dragged him to a small table in an alcove, cluttered with liquor bottles, sodas, and mixers. Plastic glasses were stacked in the corner of the table next to an ice chest that was leaking water.

"What are you drinking?" she asked.

"Soda with lime."

"Oh, come on! You need something stronger than that."

"What I need is another party. . . . All right, put some scotch in it. Here, let me do it." He took over, pouring one for her that was a little stronger.

"Are you trying to get this lady drunk?" asked a voice close behind them.

John turned to see a slender man, whom he guessed was in his early thirties. The stranger's close-cropped, salt and pepper hair was brushed back from a round, barely wrinkled face. "I think you've got it wrong," John answered. "She's trying to get ME drunk." He handed the glass to Janet and then took a sip from his own.

"Yes, I noticed you wouldn't let her pour."

"He's such a prude." Janet laughed. "But I love him anyway."

"Are you two married?" His eyes shifted back and forth.

"Oh, no." Janet felt obligated to respond. "We're just friends. He lets me tag along."

"Well, my name is Matthew." The man extended a friendly hand.

"I'm Janet."

"Hi, I'm John." The men shook hands.

"Looks like you two have been out on the town."

"Oh, these." John said, looking down at his jacket. "The ballet."

"I didn't think you'd dress just to come here. Not for one of Charles' parties anyway."

"Evidently not," he looked around.

"You know," Matthew said, speaking directly to John, "you look very familiar."

"Uh-oh." John put on his Charlie Chaplin face.

"He just has one of those profiles that's impossible to forget," Janet said teasingly.

"I thought you were going to say common."

"Not you, John. Excuse me," she said discreetly.

"Sure." John watched her fade into the crowd.

"She's very pretty," Matthew commented, also looking at her.

"Janet's a real charmer," John agreed, turning back to Matthew.

"You know, it really bothers me that I can't remember where I've seen you. I'm sure I'll remember at some unusual moment when I'm half-asleep or mowing the lawn."

"You have a house?"

"Unfortunately."

"Why do you say that?"

"Well, I had a lover and we broke up some time ago, so the house is on the market now. I'm still there."

"And your friend?"

"He's there too."

"Tends to drag things out a little, doesn't it?"

"I suppose it does. Someone I met at a friend's house was telling me. . . ." He stopped. "Do you know Bob Angstrom?"

"No."

"Well, anyway, he was saying these things take time, so I'm not going to rush it."

There was a pause. "Well, I'd better see how Janet is faring."

"Okay. Nice to see you again."

"Oh, we'll be milling about. I'll talk to you a little later."

"Good. Enjoy yourself."

John stepped into the huge living room. He felt good about having run into Matthew. He seemed warm and friendly and had remembered him from somewhere, or so he said. As for himself, John could hardly remember what he had for dinner the night before. If Matthew really had seen John before, he must have thought well of him at the time to have remembered. But then on the other hand, Matthew could have remembered because of something negative or unflattering. Although he didn't seem to be uncomfortable a moment ago. So John decided that Matthew must have liked him.

What was it that caused people to like him, he wondered as he surveyed the room. No one arrives at where they are without first travelling down many roads to get there. John's first recollections were of New York and his grandmother's house in Brooklyn. He remembered the lace doilies and the French doors that opened into the parlor and the cat that hid from him under the bed. He remembered, too, visions of dough being rolled into spaghetti and then hanging on a rack in the kitchen and the fragrance of homemade apple pie seeping into every room. He and his younger brother grew up with holiday reunions and parents who never fought, church every Sunday and television every night. His mother was beautiful and loved the theatre. She dressed up in stylish clothes, dabbled perfume behind her ears, and took them to every musical. He remembered the lavish productions, the excitement, the people buzzing about in the lobby, the anticipation on his mother's face as they were leaving for the theatre. She was so happy on those days. She had been brought up on big bands and Frank Sinatra and tried to instill her passions in her children. They would be cultured, refined—not like the punks on South Street.

His father worked at the Post office. Laughing and kind when things went well, he was stern and severe when the boys got out of hand. With a "spare the rod and spoil the child" policy, he was determined that his sons would never be spoiled. He had served in the Navy and, stationed in Key West, had fallen in love with it. When a position came up in the Miami Post Office, he applied for a transfer. Reluctantly his wife agreed to move South. She conceded that it would be good to raise the two boys in the sun; let them breathe the clean sweet breezes of the Gulfstream and savor the fragrance of tropical flowers. John knew only the wind that blew through the canyons of Manhattan and the smell of the East River. So they took him out of his New York grade school and planted him in paradise.

Those early years were seemingly idyllic. He befriended the boy across the street, had exploratory sex with him, and played in the salt air of the Atlantic Ocean. He knew nothing of finance, love was a bore, and his parents had all the answers. He didn't worry about tomorrow, nor care about yesterday. He and his brother watched as flat train cars, loaded with white missiles, passed through on their way to Key West during the Cuban Crisis. There were military convoys back then, too. Handsome chisel-faced men in green, wearing helmets with hanging straps, passed by in trucks and jeeps. They were out of place among the palm-lined boulevards and the green grass, like shepherds and Christmas angels in an air-conditioned church.

He grew to maturity wanting all of the same things other boys wanted—a house, a beautiful wife, and two kids that he could raise the way his father had raised him. But the road signs he followed led to a divided highway: his friends on one side and himself on the other. At nineteen he began to doubt the divinity of the Pope and fell from grace in his mother's eyes. But these wounds healed in time. However the next tear in the fabric of family unity almost ripped it apart. He was barely a man at twenty-one when he announced that he was moving North to be with Brad. Though his family didn't know it, Brad was John's first lover. His father felt the move would be good for him; teach him independence. He had recently discovered a whole new world of people like himself. Suddenly, he had new friends and a new beginning.

Then came the day when his father received that anonymous phone call. Years later the memory of that day still burned in John's memory. He had walked into the house with nothing on his mind except what the mailman might have brought.

"I got a phone call," his father said dryly.

"From whom?" John said casually, sorting through the envelopes on the desk.

"Someone says this man Brad, that you're going to live with, is homosexual."

The floor swerved beneath his feet. The air was completely still as he raised his eyes. His father was looking at him, waiting for his response. "Yes, that's true."

"You knew that?" his father sounded surprised.

"Yes," John walked over to the champagne-colored sofa covered in clear plastic and sat down.

"John, you don't have to go. You can stay here with us. Your room's still there for you."

"I want to go, Dad."

There was a pause as his father considered the implications of John's answer. "Does that mean you're homosexual too?"

"Yes."

"Oh, John," his father said, his voice breaking.

The fabric ripped like the rending of the curtain in the temple that separated the common people from the holy of holies. His father cried and put his arms around John. "We'll send, you to the best psychiatrists. We'll lick this thing."

Calmly, John said that he did not need a psychiatrist. Everything would be all right. Afterwards, he was amazed at the amount of control he had exhibited. Had he not been caught by surprise he might not have handled it in the same direct way. He denied nothing and at the same time did not alter his plans. The days that followed, however, were emotionally tense. It was the middle of the rainy season. The sun was hidden away for a portion of every afternoon, keeping him, his mother and brother closed together in the house for hours on end. The rains came as they did every year to interrupt the light and to nourish the seeds waiting in the earth. It was all a part of the cycle of birth, death, and rebirth so prevalent in the tropics.

During this troubled period of adjustment, his parents gradually saw that there was nothing to do but to accept John's decision, and they made no effort to change him. One day his mother confessed to him, "I was so scared that you would go away and never talk to me again."

"I could never do that, Mom," he had answered, hugging her. When he finally moved, he began a correspondence with his mother, father, and brother. He remembered the letters they received from his aunts and cousins in New York, recounting, among other things what their husbands had been doing. John tried to mimic these letters by writing about things he and Brad had done. In one letter he spoke about plans for a weekend with Brad's parents. He got a letter back, saying that they loved him very much but didn't want to hear about Brad. Walling off a part of their son, they continued to love him around it. John didn't push, but deep inside he recognized a loss and moved emotionally further and further away from them. He let them live their lives without interference, until the three of them had little in common anymore.

His parents had died seven years apart and he still cried when he thought about them. But he also came to understand that they were people, like anybody else—like him. They had wants and needs and desires and faults and expectations. He acknowledged them as human beings rather than as parent-gods.

At thirty-one, he was overly sensitive and had the virtue of being intensely disliked by no one. He always listened to people as if their problem were the only thing in his life at the moment. It was Janet who got him to begin talking about his own problems. He used to hold them inside, thinking that nobody was interested in hearing about what troubled him. He swallowed it like bitter bile to ferment within. She opened him up, made him spit it out, and saved him from himself. He never forgot that.

He looked for her in the living room, scanning the bodies standing around with cocktail glasses in one hand. She wasn't among them. He glanced forlornly about and then headed through the sliding glass doors that led onto the patio. The area was dominated by a long rectangular swimming pool filled with irridescent blue water. Beyond it was a wall of palms and tropical plants that curved in and out to allow pockets of grass and tile, where guests were standing. He found Janet at the end of a gray wooden deck that ran along the back of the house. She was leaning against a post covered by a flowering yellow Alamanda vine. Three men were gathered around her as she chattered. "Yes, a real charmer," he thought, reminded of the words he had said earlier to Matthew.

"Oh, there you are, John. This is Richard, Bill, and Ronnie." She touched the third fellow. "Ah . . . Ron. I'm sorry," she laughed. "This is Ron. Not Ronnie."

"Hi," John said and squinted at Janet, trying to detect how many drinks she'd had.

The party was lively; the people were fun; the music was incessant. From the looks of things, he needn't have worried about Janet's having a good time. Obviously, she was enjoying the party more than he was. But after a while he did manage to loosen up a bit. Charles had come over and taken his jacket and tie. Then he rolled up his sleeves, undid a few of the upper buttons, and for the first time, felt almost at ease.

Matthew had come to the party much earlier, but he had not been on time. If he had come alone he would have arrived at precisely nine o'clock. Punctuality was one of his best qualities, or so his friends said. But he didn't come alone. He was with his best friend, Carlos, and Carlos wouldn't think of

arriving anywhere on time. Laughingly, he once told Matthew
that he was operating on Cuban time, and that, he added, ran
at least two hours behind gringo time. Except for an
occasional nuance, Carlos was completely Americanized, at
least on the surface. And he was as different from Matthew as
Katherine Hepburn was from Spencer Tracy. Yet for all of
their differences, Matthew thought, as they stood next to each
other, they shared the bond of platonic friendship. Who can
say what brings people together, he mused. Was it the
similarities or the differences that cement relationships, platonic or otherwise? What for example, had brought John and
Janet together? He was Italian, she was Jewish. He was
Brooklyn, she was Long Island. He was gay, she was straight.
Yet, they were the best of friends.

Matthew retreated back to Carlos and told him about the
man in the tux. In turn, Carlos told him about the muscle man
from Key Biscayne. Their thoughts and impressions inter-
twined and mixed with the music as it surged through the
room. The evening wore on and the pulsating rhythms were
replaced by the more relaxed beat of a group from the 500
Club clustered around the piano, singing off key. The club,
which took its name from its address downtown, had been
founded by Charles as a gay resource and support center. In
addition to hosting parties like this, it sponsored dinners,
lectures, and in general assisted the gay community whenever
it could. John had only been to a few of its meetings where he
met Charles and a few other people but he had seen an ad for
the party in *The Weekly News* that headlined in bold letters,
MEET NEW FRIENDS.

John led Janet back inside to listen to the piano and they
joined Matthew and Carlos on the sofa. Nobody commented
on the chorus except Janet, who called it a cute idea. They
fancied themselves the Mormon Tabernacle Choir. More
realistically, they ressembled the crowd at O'Reiley's on a
Friday night.

The quartet on the sofa were enjoying themselves. Occasionally, they burst out singing a few bars of whatever was being pounded out of the piano and smiled at each other when they did. When the pianist finally stood up and the singing stopped, John took the opportunity to say goodnight.

"Listen," Carlos said pleasantly. "I'm having a few people over for drinks on Sunday. Why don't the two of you come?"

"That sounds nice," John said, looking at Janet for confirmation and receiving it.

"Good," Carlos reached into his right pocket and pulled out a card which he handed to John. "There's my address and the phone number in case you get lost. About nine o'clock," he said as Matthew looked on, mildly surprised. John thanked him. They exchanged good-byes, John collected his jacket and tie and escorted Janet out the front door.

2.

Carlos Montana was 29 years old, and aside from being the youngest member of his family, he was also the shortest, measuring 5'5". His black eyes and pointed brows accented the high forehead and short black hair. His angular features were softened by the round, red glasses that he always wore. His skinny frame and those long, magical fingers conjured up images of Keebler elves who lived in trees and baked cookies. Despite a certain pomposity, there was a sort of whimsical quality about him that made people love him.

Like most people his age or older, he had not been born in South Florida but had migrated there from somewhere else. Carlos had been born in Cuba, just outside of Havana. When he was two, his parents moved to the United States, where he grew up and attended private schools in Virginia.

He didn't mind the school as much as the blue uniforms they made the students wear. He wanted nothing more than to be like normal kids his age who dressed in street clothes and went to public school. Nothing more than to belong. The students he saw on television never looked like he did and he was bitterly reminded of his difference every time he put on the blue uniform. In childhood, his clothes were the visible mark of his captivity, in adulthood they became the symbol of his independence. As long as he wore that uniform he was stifled, shy, and awkward.

Then came high school and, with it, normalcy: For the

first time he was like other boys, and conformity now was both a balm to his shrunken ego and a means toward acceptance. He lost weight, and in the search for his place in the scheme of things, joined a group of intellectuals on campus. In addition to showing him the treasures of his mind, they indoctrinated him in the social arts. Suddenly, he was popular. They took him well beyond self acceptance to standing on the brink of arrogance.

His father was an engineer and he devoutly wanted Carlos to become an architect. There were visions of father and son working together to build great public structures. So Carlos entered the University of Florida, at Gainesville, to pursue a career that really didn't interest him. The same month that his father died, he switched majors. For some time he had thought about changing to city planning and political science, but had hesitated, knowing that he would have seriously disappointed his father. The older Montana's death was a release for Carlos, a chance for the young man to escape what he thought to be his inevitable fate and to follow instead a career of his own choosing.

Graduate work at the University paid off, enabling him to obtain a position with the City of Miami, commanding a salary that most men didn't see until middle age. Though free and easy in his sexual orientation, he did not permit his sexual affairs to extend into his professional life. Work was a serious business, providing money and status—the symbols of his tangible superiority. (Since his father's death, he had managed the family money and invested wisely in real estate. Though perky and flamboyant, he was surprisingly shrewd when it came to business.) Thus, professional ethics were strictly observed by him, and he never discussed sex in the office. This is not to say that those with whom he worked were ignorant of his orientation. Carlos could never hide, nor ever wish to hide, his rather middle-of-the-road masculinity. At the office it was simply irrelevant.

Carlos' propensity for the finer things carried over into his homelife. His two-story town house was tastefully decorated. The gray walls of the living room were hung with quiet, modern prints, framed in chrome and spotlighted from above. The conversation pit, where Carlos exhibited his social talents, had two love seats flanked by a Barcelona chair. Around them, smaller chairs were randomly placed to handle any overflow. A thick glass table tied it all together. If, by some remote chance, a guest were left unattended, there were ample copies of *Architectural Digest* neatly arranged on the coffee table to amuse him.

The two bedrooms upstairs afforded more than enough space, if Randy could ever be convinced to move in. But Randy was not the marrying kind. So, brooding over Randy's disdain for monogamy, Carlos took advantage of whatever opportunities were at hand. He was popular and had no trouble making friends, especially if he had had a drink or two to smooth his way.

Sunday night came quickly and Carlos wiped a patch of dust from the bookcase as he waited for his friends to appear.

The bar was well stocked and everything was in its proper place. The two art deco lamps glowed softly, light jazz drifted in from somewhere, and the front door had a sign hung on it that read, 'This is the place.'

As usual, Matthew was the first to arrive, followed soon by Randy, with a friend, a tall slender man with steel blue eyes and dirty blonde hair. Carlos greeted his current love with his usual direct vigor. John was the last to arrive, and he was alone. He made apologies for Janet who was meeting her boy friend's family that evening.

"Oh, okay," Carlos said. "We'll see her another time. Come on in. You remember Matthew from the other night," he said, smiling.

"Hi."

"That's my friend, Randy, and this is Bob."

"Hi," John repeated.

"You didn't tell us what your name was," Randy said.

"I'm sorry. It's John."

"No need for you to be sorry," Matthew said. "It's this one here who should be sorry." He pointed to Carlos.

"Never mind the jokes," Carlos said. "What are you drinking, dear?"

"Soda please," John replied, looking around him.

"Sit down. I'll get you some."

John paused, then pulled a chair over and sat down next to Bob. Matthew was sitting in one of the love seats. Carlos, when he wasn't pouring, joined Randy in the opposite one. Bob and John had smaller chairs that formed the bottom of the 'U'. John did not feel uncomfortable, in his jeans and heavy work shoes. "I really like what you've done with your place, Carlos," he commented appreciatively. "You must have a flair for this sort of thing."

"Please don't tell me I should have been an interior decorator," Carlos said, laughing. "That's the first assumption people make. Even the ones who've never seen my apartment."

"I think that one of the greatest adventures is to take a barren, lifeless space and transform it into your own personal domain," John continued.

"Carlos is very good at changing things," Randy said in a tone of voice that made Carlos look at him questioningly.

"It's a reflection of your inner nature, so to speak. I can look around here and tell just what kind of a person you are," John said, looking at the bookshelves.

"Well, please don't tell the others," Carlos replied archly.

"The truth comes out in the strangest places," Bob added. "Even when you try to repress it."

"That sounds exactly like something a psychiatrist would say," Matthew joined in.

"The room speaks very well of you, actually." John tried to alter the direction of the conversation that his own comments had started.

"Thank you," Carlos said, closing his eyes and nodding affirmatively at Matthew. "I just bought the most beautiful down comforter to match the violet walls in my bedroom." He paused, then said quietly to Randy, "We can test it out tonight even though I'm sure we won't need a comforter to keep us warm."

Randy blinked his eyes more than once and finally said, "Not tonight, Carlos. I have to take Bob home, remember?"

"That's all right," Carlos persisted. "I don't mind waiting. Matthew and I will probably be chatting into the wee hours."

"I'm sure you will," Randy said a little awkwardly. "Maybe some other time."

Carlos' face changed. More observant than most, Matthew was aware of the tension between Carlos and Randy. With delicate fingers, Carlos picked up his glass and drained the last of his bourbon. Then getting up, he said coolly to Bob, "Maybe you'll have better luck," and walked to the counter to put some ice in his glass.

"Me?" Bob protested. "How did I get pulled into this?"

"You're just an innocent bystander," Matthew agreed. "The poor guy is just sitting here minding his own business."

"John, how's your soda?" the host called from the bar.

"I could use a little more, I guess."

"I've been here less than an hour and already I'm a home wrecker," Bob said undeterred, to Randy.

"Don't worry about it," Randy responded, wanting to drop the whole subject.

"Stay there," Carlos said, as he brought the bottle over and poured for John. "Just kidding, Bob," he added smoothly. "How's your drink?"

Matthew watched his friend's face and knew that he hadn't been kidding at all. In fact, during that one moment, he had probably expressed his true feelings but was now able to reclaim the facade of gracious host.

"Fine, thanks," Bob replied.

The expression on Randy's face was more naked as he watched Carlos return the bottle to the bar. Pure loathing was visible on it. Meanwhile, John tried not to show too much interest in the man with steel blue eyes sitting on his right. He made the effort to become engrossed in the general conversation. He engaged the others in talk about theatre and the state of the world just enough to let them know that he was not monopolizing Bob. Yet, as he talked with Matthew, he found himself stealing glances at Bob to make sure that he was still there. Maybe he could take Bob into the corner so that the others wouldn't interrupt. But then he dismissed the thought. There was a magnetism about the tall blonde man, and John wondered if he had this effect on everybody. "So you're a psychiatrist," he said finally, looking directly into those blue eyes.

"I'm afraid so."

"Do you find yourself analyzing people, like at cocktail parties?"

Bob smiled. "I try not to. It's tough, though, sometimes."

"You don't carry a set of wallet-size Rorschachs, do you?"

"No, but we could do word-associations if you like."

"Oh, no. Not on our first date."

To John's relief, Bob laughed. "And what do you do, John?"

"Commercial art. I do things like brochures, book covers, pamphlets, all of that stuff that nobody reads."

"I really envy you your talent. I can't even draw a straight line."

Matthew chimed in. "And I'll bet that's the only thing John does that's straight!"

John looked at his smiling face and couldn't help laughing. There was a pause, and then Randy broke up the circle by saying he'd better shove off. Carlos gave him a curt, glad-to-be-rid-of-you, "O.K."

"You ready, Bob?" Randy asked as he stood up.

"Yeah, I guess so." He turned to John and said, "It was nice to meet you, and I hope I see you again."

John felt he had to act now or never. Somehow he got up the nerve to say, "Can I give you my phone number?"

"Let me get you a pad," Carlos said triumphantly and vanished off into the kitchen before Bob had a chance to protest. He was back in a minute with a small pad and pencil. John scribbled his number on the pad and ripped off the page. Giving it to Bob he added, "I'm usually there after six. By the way, what's your last name?"

"Angstrom, like in science class."

"English?"

"Swedish."

"I should have guessed. Well . . . good night."

"I'll give you a call," Bob said quietly. Then he looked beyond John and called, "Good night, Matthew."

"Bye."

Carlos escorted them both to the door. There were a few muffled good-byes, the door closed, and Carlos came back with his hands on his hips. "Can you believe that?" he shouted.

"What," Matthew asked, "that Randy left, or that he left with Bob?"

"It's the second time this week that he's had other plans."

"Are he and Bob having a fling?" John asked reluctantly.

Matthew raised his eyes as he looked at Carlos.

"No, I don't think so," Carlos said. "He's not his type."

"You weren't so sure earlier," Matthew said.

"I was pissed."

"I know you were."

"I have to be honest," Carlos said, looking depressed. "Monogamy is a real issue with me. I mean, let's face it; I want to get married. Randy knows that. We had a long talk."

"You told him you wanted to marry him?" John asked in astonishment.

"Yes, I did. I told him what I wanted right up front. I was honest."

"Sometimes honesty is scary," Matthew said.

"I'll say. You gotta work into these things gradually, with a little tact," John said in agreement.

"To hell with tact. I told him what I was feeling. If he can't deal with it, then let him find someone who wants to play games. You see, he wants it all. He wants me, but he wants to play around too."

"You don't play around?" Matthew tested.

"Sure I do. But it's not what I want. If Randy would make some kind of a commitment, I would be faithful to him."

"Is this Carlos I'm listening to?"

"Listen, honey, just because I wear red high heels doesn't mean I'm not a woman of quality."

"Oh, barf, gag, cough!" Matthew was stretched out on the sofa clutching at his throat.

John was delighted. "Red high heels?" he repeated.

"Carlos has this fantasy. He's always wanted to dress in red high heels and long white gloves."

"Of course, darlings, only the best. Quality speaks for itself. I want a little pill box hat too, you know, the one with the mesh veil."

"Yes," John said delightedly. "I can see you going to the P.T.A."

"That's right, or the ladies' auxiliary. That's it," Carlos sat up straight, "the three of us can be the ladies' auxiliary. We'll meet every Wednesday."

"Wait a minute," John protested. "I'm not a lady."

"Yes, you are. Why else are you hiding behind those construction boots?"

John laughed to hide his embarrassment.

"Don't fight it," Matthew advised. "It'll be easier if you humor him."

From the tape deck came the twang of a guitar, backed up by a full orchestra and Juice Newton started to sing *Break It To Me Gently*.

Carlos became sullen again. "I love this song." His eyes became glazed. Matthew got up and walked over to him. They stood embracing.

John was moved, but remained silent as Carlos cried.

"I'm sorry, John," he said finally, still sobbing and holding onto Matthew, "I'm not always like this."

"That's okay," John said empathetically.

"Don't worry about it," Matthew said, rubbing Carlos' delicate frame. "We're here to help each other."

"Thanks guys," Carlos sniffled, regaining his composure. Then sitting back down on the sofa he said, "I guess this was the first meeting of the L.A.s"

"L.A.s?" John asked quizzically.

"The ladies' auxilliary."

"Oh, that!"

3.

He had a distinguished look about him; but at the same time, Matthew Griffin was extremely casual, as though he were trying to conceal a rigid, nose-to-the-grindstone past. A financial exectutive for the Internal Revenue Service, he preferred to dress in old jeans and white tennis shoes. He resembled the photograph of an author one might see on the back of a 1940s novel: one with a tweed coat, patches on the elbows (Matthew was still wearing them), a button-down collar, an Irish walking hat, and a pipe dangling from his lips.

In fact, that calm exterior did not come naturally, but was the medal of valor bestowed upon him by a past filled with obstacles and uncertainty. He was reared in East Meadow, Long Island, by a frail mother who wore polka-dot dresses with lace collars. He punished her, as children will do, by setting the house on fire with his chemistry set, by telephoning her from the extension and hanging up, and by any of a number of very aggravating but totally satisfying pranks. In return she put him in the cold dark cellar and left him there, until, terrified by the rats, he begged for forgiveness.

"Why do you do these things?" she asked. "I'm your mother. You're supposed to love your mother."

"I love you, mom."

"Then why do you make me put you in the cellar? I hate doing that."

"I'm sorry."

"Oh, Matthew. What am I going to do with you?" and then she would hold him against her starched, polka-dot dress and stroke the back of his head.

The few times that Matthew saw him, his father was either drunk or unresponsive, but he did provide them with the props necessary for a respectable family image. After all, that was the reason they moved out of the city and into the picture-postcard house next to the Jones'.

His mother died when Matthew was twelve and everything changed. In some inexplicable way, he held her responsible for leaving him and his younger sister alone with a man they hardly knew. She had abandoned him to a life the boy was unprepared to accept. Rescue of sorts came when his older brother, who was 18, took an emergency leave from the Navy, and moved with the children to a one-bedroom apartment in Farmingdale. While his brother worked to support the three of them and went to school at night, Matthew ran the house and acted as parent to his sister. There was no adolescence for him. He went directly from childhood to adulthood, from living under the wing of his mother who did everything for him, to accepting the responsibilities of a grown man raising a child. At twelve years old there was no choice. There was only what was. It never occurred to him not to do it.

"It wasn't so bad," he had told John and Carlos when they agreed to get together at the 500 Club on the Wednesday night after Carlos' party. "At least I didn't think it was back then. Just a part of growing up, I figured. But I never forgave my mother."

"How could you be mad at someone for dying? God!" Carlos said accusingly.

"I was just a kid, what do you want?"

"I mean, your own mother," Carlos persisted.

"Listen, someone else is going to die in about two minutes if he doesn't shut up."

Carlos clamped his lips and looked at John for sympathy. Each of them had come out to look for something. John was hoping to get a glimpse of Bob but he soon learned that Bob's attendance at the 500 Club was sporadic. Carlos had hopes of seeing his muscle-man from Key Biscayne who did show up with a date of equally dazzling proportions. And, once again, Matthew tried in vain to figure out where he had seen John before.

"Did you go to school down here?" Matthew asked, trying to get a lead.

"For the most part, I did," John said. "Started out at Dade and finished up in France."

"Pardonnez-Moi," Carlos said.

John's response made Matthew dismiss the idea that they had met in school. He had gone to a community college in Setauket and then moved to Greenwich Village to attend the New School for Social Research. He had taken a room in the house of an old aunt who owned a brownstone on 10th Street. She lived alone and was glad to have Matthew stay with her. After he graduated, he took a job with Chase Manhattan. Life in the Village was stimulating, and though there was ample opportunity to become submerged in the gay subculture, he had remained apart. He did not frequent the bars or walk the piers where boys stood waiting for sex in the shadows. His life was the dull existence of an accountant who was never late for work. Long hours in starched white shirts, plain ties, and Mennen After Shave. He never sought out a lover or even thought of a time when love would be his. It belonged to another class of people whose lives he never touched.

And then he met Larry Alzeski from the title search department. At first it was casual—extended talks about things of no concern. The context of their words was not important, only that they were together in the same room looking into each other's eyes trying to read the hidden messages there and accidently brushing arms. Matthew remembered the tingle he felt whenever they touched. Soon it was lunches together, then dinners, and eventually that all-encompassing night in Larry's apartment when he found love. They took an apartment together in Queens, where Larry's parents lived, and vacationed in Fort Lauderdale in the winter. "The worst feeling in the world," Larry said, "was driving to Miami International with the windows open to get on a plane bound for frozen slush and gray skies." He talked about a change. Matthew was hesitant but willing to accomodate the only man he'd ever loved. He left Chase Manhattan, the theatre district, his Mahjong group, and the roots of a lifetime, for a small apartment in North Miami where the summer heat was blistering and the roaches were as big as mice.

The first year was unbearable. He couldn't get used to the change. But he had Larry and the obligation that a relationship incurred. He was committed to making it work. He would not desert his love the way his mother had deserted him. And he would be there to listen when he was needed the way his father never did. He would not inflict upon another human being the pain that he had endured.

Things were going well. They both had good jobs. The years passed gracefully. They settled into their lives together. No longer a seasonal resort, Miami had grown since their arrival. Well-to-do Cubans were taking up residence as well as Canadians and the elderly from the great Northeast. It was the playground of New York and was sometimes referred to as "the sixth borough." Condominiums were growing like huge mushrooms out of the palm-laden landscape. Beaches were eroding, and utopia was being paved over with white highways. Land values were on the rise. It was time to buy a house, a place of their own, where Matthew could carry out his conjugal obligations, those mystical rites of devotion that would somehow make up for his imperfect childhood.

But after ten years, passion turned to mutual respect, and

excitement once again became the province of another class of people whose lives he never touched. But Matthew was not a sexual animal, and he was content in his routine. Larry was not so content, and ever so subtly a crevice opened between them and widened. Larry needed the fulfillment that his lover no longer provided. At first he agonized over his desires, certain that they were unwholesome, and condemned himself to a life of secret indulgence. He was like a starving man paralyzed by guilt over the stealing of a slice of bread. Matthew had, at some level, been aware of the changes, though he didn't fully admit it to himself. There was nothing to substantiate his suspicions and he felt ashamed at being jealous and untrusting. All he had were vague feelings, unfamiliar scents, and hang-up phone calls. Yet the notion that something was wrong began to obsess him, and he slipped into a continuous state of melancholy. He was afraid that he was failing, that his marriage, the only salvation given to him for his miserable childhood, would not be enough. Beelzebub had scored another point by showing Matthew how to reconcile the past, and then snatching the opportunity away. It wasn't fair.

He was despondent and living only by habit. He didn't laugh. He didn't cry. He only worked and took tranquilizers that the doctor prescribed. He lived apart from himself, separate from his emotions, until that day he caught Larry in his bed with some poor kid from Hollywood. Then his fury was unleashed and all of that anger and resentment came pouring down like the fires over Sodom. Five days later he attempted suicide with tranquilizers.

The relationship of so many years had ended, or at least assumed another level of existance. For practical purposes, they decided to stay together in the house. It was during this time that Matthew began formulating new concepts about the nature of his life. Having reached an impasse, he changed direction. He became aware of different ideas stirring within

him waiting to be acknowledged, notions born of the profound experience of a close convergence with death. One of
these new ideas was a realization that life was nothing more
than what he created, and that whether he found himself in
the brightest heaven or in the darkest hell was dependent
wholly upon his own actions. God himself would not attempt
to interfere. It was during this time also that Matthew went
out to Karleman's Bar in an effort to break away from Larry
and to meet new people—people who would relate to him as
an individual and not as one half of a relationship.

One night he stood by the telephone at the side of the bar
near a man in a green polo shirt leaning against the thin
counter that ran the length of the wall. Matthew looked over a
few times, trying to decide whether or not to risk saying hello.
After being out of circulation for so long, he felt uncomfortable. Here he was single again and back in the bars, alone.
Again. He hated it. But that was the way it worked. There
was no way around it. If he wanted to meet people, this was
what he had to do.

Only a week before, he had attended a fund-raiser for the
Coalition for Human Rights and was transfixed by a boy
sitting by himself reading a flyer on the other side of the room.
A friend had said to him, "You're being very obvious about
this."

Matthew said, "I don't care if I'm being obvious. I just
want to look at him."

"Well, why don't you go over and talk to him?"

"Now you're asking the impossible. I can't just walk up
to someone I don't know and start a conversation. What am I
going to say after I say hello?"

Eventually, the boy got up and left.

And now, only a short time afterwards, he was faced
with the same dilemma. If he said nothing, the man would
leave as sure as the boy with the flyer left. But if he said,
"hello," then there was the chance for something unknown.

He took a deep breath, looked over to his left and said, "How are you doing tonight?" Even as he spoke, he wondered how he would react if his question were ignored.

To Matthew's relief, the man smiled and said, "Fine, how about you?"

He'd done it. The way was clear for further conversation. The knot loosened in his stomach. "Good," he said, nodding.

"The music's pretty good tonight." The man straightened up and moved closer to Matthew.

"Yes, it is," Matthew agreed, not knowing whether it was or not, but feeling safe in the assumption.

"Are you from around here?" the man asked with interest.

"Oh, yes. I live about two miles away."

"Thought you might have been a tourist."

"Not this time. Actually, I've been here about ten years. My lover and I bought a place." He wondered if he had said too much but realized he would have to say something if he was going to invite the man home since Larry would probably be there.

"You have a lover?" came the expected invitation to explain.

"Well, not anymore. We just broke up." Matthew felt his chances slipping away with each word.

"I see. How long were you together?" he asked as if he were actually interested.

"Almost fourteen years."

"That's a long time. It must be difficult for you," the man said.

"Yes, it is. But there are other things to consider."

"Like what?"

"Like the possibility of meeting other people, nice people." Matthew was tempted to say, "like you," but caught himself.

"I guess it's like starting all over again."

"Yes." There was a pause while they listened to the music. Then Matthew leaned over and said, "What's your name?"

"John," he said. "What's yours?"

Matthew told him and then invited him back to the house.

John flinched. He had had too many experiences with people on the rebound. He was determined not to let that happen again, no matter how interesting or attractive they were. "Not this time," he said, putting his empty glass on the counter. "I think I'm going to head on home." And with that, John awkwardly left the bar.

John's office was located on the 25th floor of a mirror and concrete structure that loomed over Flagler Street in the heart of downtown Miami. During the daytime the street was crowded with people moving in every direction. The smell of Café con Leche mingled with street garbage, perfume, and horse droppings graciously left by the beasts of the mounted police. American executives and Coast Guard men in uniforms moved side by side with tourists from Columbia, Peru, Guatemala, and Brazil. Cubans stood in their store fronts and grimaced when anyone spoke to them in English. Japanese boys rushed by carrying cameras from their homeland and sporting backpacks. Fashion-conscious secretaries passed by bag ladies, pushing their fortunes around in shopping carts. It was truly America's melting pot. In the middle of all of this, John carried out his trade. He had his own small office in the public affairs branch of a large corporation. A second artist had the office next to his, and beyond that was the photo lab.

The walls of John's office were covered with sheets of typestyles, posters, a map of the New York subway system, and original cards sent to him by Janet through inter-office mail from the sixth floor. He sat at a drawing table, which took up half the office. It was covered with papers, drawings, triangles, and a long metal T-square. A credenza with a file drawer that took up the wall to the right of the table was cluttered with rows of colored markers, books, a coffee cup, and various small items that seemed to be there out of default.

There were footsteps in the hall. A shadow appeared in his doorway and knocked on the wall. He looked up. "Hi, Janet. Come on in."

"I was just in the neighborhood, so I thought I'd stop by to see you and your beautiful view. Gloria said you were here."

"That Gloria lets anybody in."

"Oh you love it when I come to visit because it keeps 'em guessing."

"It's always nice to see a friendly face from the sixth floor. They're usually so grim down there."

She gave him a mock smile. "Are you working on my report cover?"

"Not today. That's only a rush; this is an emergency."

"Did I pick a bad time?" She sounded concerned.

"Not at all, they loosened the shackles this morning. Sit down." He cleared three lay-outs from the black-and-chrome chair.

"I'll go ahead and take that cover back since I'll have some time this afternoon," Janet said, pulling her skirt beneath her.

"Good, then I can talk to you for awhile. Would you like some coffee?" His eyebrows went up.

"No thank you."

"Perhaps I could interest you in a few truffles?"

"Are they fresh?" She looked at him out of the corners of her eyes.

"We just put the pigs away."

"That's all right. I think I'll pass."

"You look very nice this morning."

"Are you kidding? I look hideous. This hair," she said, exasperated.

"Makes you look sensual."

"Oh, thank you." She pulled at the thin material on her arms. "I wore this dress today because it has long sleeves."

"Is that to hide the needle marks?"

"As a matter of fact, it is. I went to see my allergist yesterday. . . ."

"And he said there's nothing wrong with me." John quoted the old introduction to "Doctor's Orders".

"I'm just missin' my man," they recited together.

"Actually, my allergist gave me the shots. It still hurts. I feel like a beekeeper with a hole in his asbestos. I've got this awful welt on my arm."

"Where is it, the left arm?"

"Yes, right here," she said, rubbing.

"Well, at least you can still draw. Do you think it'll stop the sniffles?"

"I hope so," she drawled. "It's costing me a week's pay."

"Ooh. I wonder if I should have myself tested for allergies? I'm always catching cold. At least, I think they're colds. Maybe they're allergies."

"He's very good. I'll have to give you his number later."

"You realize, of course, that we sound like a couple of yentas sitting around talking about our aches and pains."

"I know." She touched her cheek.

"How did your dinner go with Anton's parents?"

"It was very nice," she brightened. "I was so nervous at first. You know, meeting the parents and all. That's a big step."

"It is." John shook his head in agreement.

"But they liked me, or at least they pretended to."

"I'm sure they did. How could they help loving you?"

"You're too good. Naturally, we had lasagne."

"That's right, they're Italian."

"I've always been attracted to Italian men," she said.

"That's just simple good taste. Is Anton first generation American?"

"Almost. He came here when he was six."

"Really? That's why he has an accent."

"You should hear his parents. I had to keep my dictionary handy right through the after-dinner brandy. And speaking of drinks. . . ."

"Yes?"

"I must have had more than I'm used to. The next day was awful. I was afraid to ask Anton if I behaved myself. His parents are very strict, you know."

"That reminds me of the time we smoked that pot from the pineapple. Remember, we filled it with rum and pulled the smoke through?"

"Oh, yes. How could I forget?"

"I really got wiped out on that. Wasn't that the night I couldn't go home and had to sleep on your couch?"

"No, John, that was another time. That was when we went to see Brenda and her parrot."

"Coconut!"

"Right." She nodded and pointed her finger at the same time. "We all sat around and got high; you, me, Brenda, and Coconut. Then, when we came back to my apartment, I had to walk you up the stairs, you poor thing."

"I'm sure the neighbors had a lot to talk about that night."

"Are you kidding? I never see my neighbors. I don't even know who lives in the apartment two doors down. I wouldn't worry about it."

"Well, I'm not doing that anymore," John said.

"Smoking, you mean?"

"Any of it. I'm trying to detoxify."

"You didn't smoke that much in the first place." She

wagged her head at him. "I think that's one of the reasons it affected you so strongly. If you were doing it every day, you wouldn't have gotten such a reaction."

"I know, but Janet, you have to remember that I've been doing poppers for ten years, too, and all that shit's still in my body. Maybe that's why I was catching colds. All I had to do was share an elevator with someone who had the sniffles, and wouldn't you know it?"

"Really!"

"But, ever since the day that I freaked out here at the office, I've been trying to get my body back in shape."

"I remember that," she said soberly. "You stormed into my office and couldn't sit still for five minutes. I couldn't even talk to you, and I didn't have any valium. I felt so helpless. . . . If you want to detox, though, I know what you should do," she said, raising her eyebrows.

"What's that?"

"It sounds really gross but it works."

"Tell me. I can handle it."

"I'll tell you only because you and I can talk about things that I wouldn't dare say to anyone else."

"What?" he pleaded.

"Coffee enemas." She enunciated carefully.

"Oh . . . you're right. It does sound gross."

She started laughing, "I told you." She bent her hand at the wrist.

"Why coffee enemas?"

"Because, the caffeine is absorbed by your liver, but the liver rejects it and spits out all of the junk and other toxic material that it's been collecting at the same time. So it cleans out your liver. Not a very lovely process, I grant you, but if it works . . . I mean, if I can go through these allergy shots, you can take a simple coffee enema."

"Simple, huh? No, it sounds interesting. I'm not doubting you. I've just never heard of it. What do I do, just let it sit there?"

"Put the coffee in the bag—you'll have to get an enema kit—and let it flow in while you're lying on your left side."

"Yeah?" His forehead wrinkled.

"Stay there for about five minutes; then lie on your back for another five minutes and then on your right side."

"So it's fifteen minutes," he said stupidly.

"Yes, then eliminate it in the bathroom, and that's it."

"And you say that will help me detoxify?"

"It should. The liver stores all that gunk, so if you clean that out you're detoxing."

"How do you know all this?"

"Oh, I'm full of all sorts of medical trivia."

"I doubt that *General Hospital* would back you up on this one, Janet."

"You're probably right. But I don't think doctors know that much about natural healing and prevention. They're more concerned with symptoms, and unless you come down with something, they're not going to be much help. Try it. It won't hurt you and it might help."

"I don't know. I'll probably stick to more conventional methods."

"Just stay straight?"

"Not that conventional."

She laughed. "I meant abstinence."

"Right. What really gets me mad at myself is that I still take it when someone offers me the stuff. Whether they're passing the joint or the little bottle, it doesn't matter."

"Well, you've only begun to get off it. Takes time to change."

"I guess."

There was a pause then Janet asked. "By the way, how was your evening with those two guys we met at the party?"

"Oh, Matthew and Carlos. That's right, I haven't talked to you for a while. It was very nice. I had a good time."

"I'm sorry I wasn't able to go. I hope they didn't think I was making excuses."

"No. I told them you were meeting potential in-laws. They understood completely."

"That's good. How many people were there?"

"Just five. I met someone interesting though."

"Really?"

"A psychiatrist."

"How convenient."

"Couldn't keep my eyes off him. Tall, thin, charming."

"Sounds delectable. Did you make a date?"

"I was very assertive. You would have been proud of me. I gave him my phone number . . . but he hasn't called."

"Isn't that always the way?"

"The weekend is coming again, so I've got my fingers crossed. I find it amazing that you can live in a town for such a long time and go out to all of the places that everyone else goes to and still meet people that you've never seen before."

"I know," she agreed.

"I think he's been to the 500 Club, but I haven't seen him there. Not that I've been going that long, myself. At least he wasn't there last Wednesday."

"Well, I'm sure he'll show up eventually," she said, standing up. "I've got to get back downstairs before they realize how long I've been gone. I drove out to the Hialeah office. And I have some news for you. They drive like maniacs out there even when it's not rush hour."

John rolled his chair back. "You know, I overheard two ladies talking the other day as we waited at an intersection for the walk sign. One of them said she didn't know why they drive like that and the other one, who had an accent, said it was because all of the people who couldn't pass the road test in Cuba had licenses to drive in Miami."

"The price you pay for living in the city. I've got to go."

"Don't forget your cover." He handed her three sheets of paper clipped together.

"Thanks a lot," she said sarcastically.

He raised his eyebrows and watched her leave, then turned back to the table and lined up his T-square.

4.

Matthew had gone out to a fast food restaurant and decided that he would stop in to see Carlos. He pulled the car into a gas station, walked into the phone booth, and fumbled for a quarter to put in the slot. With steady fingers, he dialed the number that he knew by heart. After a few rings, Carlos answered and told Matthew that he didn't have to call from a pay phone and that he should come on over. He wasn't doing anything but watching a production of the ballet *The Sleeping Beauty* on public television.

It took five minutes for Matthew to reach his friend's door. Carlos kissed him in. The television screen showed the good fairies bestowing their gifts upon a newly christened Princess Aurora.

"Did you talk to Randy?" Matthew said dropping onto one of the love seats. He stretched his legs out in front of him and got comfortable.

"Not since the other day when you were here," Carlos said, sitting in the other loveseat. "He left in a huff, so I'm not going to call him."

"Well, it's only been a few days. He'll call, don't worry."

"Oh, I'm not worried," Carlos said, cooly. Then he softened, "I don't know: sometimes I wish he wouldn't. I wish the whole thing were over and done."

"I know the feeling." Matthew sharply drew in his breath a couple of times and then sneezed.

"Are you coming down with something?"

"No, no. Sinuses. When I change from outside to inside or when I get nervous."

"You sneeze when you get nervous?" Carlos was amazed. "You must be a real joy on a first date. Let me get you something to keep you calm." He waddled into the kitchen. "Bourbon?"

"Fine. Put an ice cube in, will you?"

"Coming right up," Carlos said, opening the freezer. "You know, I think sometimes that Randy is jealous." He dropped two ice cubes into a glass.

"Of what?"

"This may sound a little far-fetched," Carlos said, "but I think he's jealous of you."

"You're right; that does sound far-fetched."

"You know how much time we spend together," he said, handing Matthew the drink and sitting opposite him.

"My God. That's like being jealous of your brother or something."

"Isn't it?"

"I think you're reading into this."

"Maybe, but just the same. If he comes into the bar when we're there, we'll split up for awhile."

"Carlos, that's ridiculous. You're going just a little overboard. He's gonna see me there eventually."

"Yes, but it won't be like we're together all the time."

"Carlos, I'm not going to hide in a corner."

"You don't have to hide in a corner. Anywhere, as long as we're not next to each other."

"No. Absolutely not."

There was a knock at the door. "Who the hell is that?" Carlos walked over slowly while Matthew sipped his bourbon and watched the ballet. The wicked fairy, Carabosse, entered the castle furious that she was not invited to the christening.

Carlos opened the door a crack to see who was there. His eyes popped open in surprise.

"Randy," he said nervously. "What are you doing here?"

"Well, I was on my way home and thought I'd stop in." The words had a hollow sound.

"Oooh, how nice." Carlos' face was still between door and jam.

"Actually, I came out to talk to you." Carlos said nothing and waited. "Can I come in?"

"Ah, yes . . . You can," he paused, "as soon as I take the eggs off the stove." He closed the door and pressed the button in the knob. He twirled around to Matthew, a look of pain on his face. "It's Randy!" he whispered desperately.

"So? Let him in."

"I can't."

"Why not?"

"He can't see you here."

"Why? Am I invisible?"

"Matthew, I want you to hide."

"I will not!"

"Please. This is important. If you're my friend you'll do this for me. Just for a little while."

"Carlos!"

"Please."

"Okay. I don't feel right doing this," Matthew said reluctantly. "I'll go upstairs."

"No. I just painted the floors."

"Painted them?" Matthew questioned, putting his glass on the dinning room table.

"Yes, in marble tile."

"How interesting, I'd . . ."

"Quick, in here." Carlos opened a door next to the stairs.

"Oh, no. Not the closet!"

"It'll only be for a little while. I promise." A knock at the door. "Please." He pushed Matthew in before his friend could protest.

"I'll never forgive you for this, Carlos," came a muffled cry.

"Sshhh." He fixed his hair, adjusted his glasses, smiled, and quietly opened the door. "Randy. It's good to see you."

"What's going on?"

"Nothing. My eggs were getting hard."

"Eggs at nine o'clock in the evening?"

"I enjoy them any time."

"Oh. Well, go ahead. I can talk while you eat."

"I already did. Eat. They were very little eggs."

Randy raised his eyebrows but didn't bother pursuing the subject any further. "I wanted to clear up a few things that we talked about. I didn't really have an answer for you at the time, but, as I thought about it, a few things occurred to me."

"That sounds great and I'd love to talk about it. Why don't we go out somewhere?"

"What's the matter with right here?"

"Oh, it's so stuffy in here and it smells like . . . burnt eggs," Carlos said, waving his hand in the air as if he were fanning away smoke.

"Burnt? I thought you ate them."

"Well, I did, but they were burnt when I ate them."

"Carlos, I don't know what's going on with you tonight."

"Nothing. Nothing is going on. I don't see anything unusual." He gulped Matthew's bourbon.

"You shouldn't drink when you're alone. It's a sign of dependency."

"Oh, I don't. Only when I'm going to eat something. Helps me digest, you know."

"Eggs and whiskey?"

"Bourbon."

"Eeecht." Randy walked over to the sliding glass door that overlooked the patio and stared out into the darkness. "I don't think that it's right that you should demand so much of me when you don't even live up to your own standards."

"What do you mean?" Carlos said, still standing by the table.

"Monogamy! You expect me to be seeing only you, but at the same time you're going out with every Tom, Dick, and Harry."

The waltz from the ballet began, and Carlos suddenly remembered the lyrics from the Disney version "Some Day My Prince Will Come."

"That's because I'm frustrated. You're the only one that means anything to me, Randy. I'm not serious about any of the others. I don't even know their names."

"Oh, no?" Randy said ominously.

"That's right."

"And what about Matthew?"

"What about Matthew?" Carlos said haughtily.

"Don't tell me that nothing is going on between you two."

A monster of a sneeze came from the closet.

"Bless you," Randy said still looking out over the garden, deep in thought.

"Thank you," Carlos replied. "There's nothing going on between me and Matthew. Oh, those eggs, I just can't stand the smell anymore. We're going out for a drink and discuss this like two reasonable adults."

Randy turned around and looked at Carlos. "If it'll make you feel more at ease, we'll go. You're as nervous as a caterpillar at a bird convention."

"Yes, it really would make me feel much better. I'll get my umbrella."

Randy raised his eyebrows. "It's not raining."

"Well, you never know with this Florida weather," Carlos said, carefully opening the closet door a fraction and thanking God that it opened away from Randy. Matthew handed him the umbrella. "Lock the door when you leave," he whispered. Matthew nodded with a frown.

"What?" Randy said, walking back towards his friend.

Carlos slammed the closet shut. "Lock the door. I've got to remember to lock the door."

"Oh yeah," Randy grunted as he walked out.

Carlos followed, sighing with relief as he shut the front door behind him.

5.

It was a safe five days before Bob called. John had begun to wonder if it had been another meaningless exchange of telephone numbers. When he heard the voice on the other end, he recognized it immediately. Bob said that he was free tonight and wondered if they could get together for dinner. John had thought of going out with Carlos and Matthew later, but did not hesitate to accept Bob's invitation. This man was hardly as accessible as his friends. They agreed on a time and hung up. John immediately jumped off the sofa. An hour and a half to get the apartment looking as though it were kept in a state of perpetual clean, take his second shower, and get dressed. The last two could be done in twenty-five minutes, but the apartment—getting that in any order would take all of the time he could spare even though it was only a studio. He had let the place go since the weekend, rationalizing that he was a creative spirit and creative spirits don't live in organized spaces. They were more concerned with less tangible issues that transcended last night's dirty dishes. Appearances were unimportant, unless, of course, you had a date in ninety minutes.

The studio was small. It used to be the garage, and stuck out of the side of a grand, two-story house in the old section of Coral Gables. The Spanish architecture was typical for the area. The stuccoed walls were painted flamingo, and a barrel tile roof kept it cool in the summer. The house was set back from the orchid trees that lined Sidonia Avenue by a lawn of thick green grass. John had an agreement with the landlady to maintain the grounds in exchange for a reduced rent payment, a job that he thoroughly enjoyed. Working in the yard was pleasantly calming—a way of getting closer to nature. He loved to mold the earth, nurture it, and make it grow. The huge tropical banana leaves that shaded his door flourished because of his own skill. He had played a part in creation.

It wasn't the first time he had managed a yard. When his mother died he received enough money to put a down payment on a two-bedroom house with a pool in Fort Lauderdale. The neighborhood was questionable, but the house was ideal. He moved in and set about transforming the grounds, adding shrubs, trees, and land works. He mowed the lawn and clipped the hedges, and everyone said he was going to raise the taxes if he did any more. His home was his sanctuary, and he wanted it to be a shining example of beauty and life in the tropics.

But the sanctuary had been defiled. Two months after he moved in, it was broken into by drugged thieves who beat him and left him lying on his living room floor. He got a broken bone out of it, the thieves got a stereo. When they found out that he was gay, the sheriff's deputies accused him of picking up his assailant, and instead of helping him prosecute, they sent him away confused and humiliated. But as an artist, he understood that sensitivity was born of insensitivity and character was one of the few good things that arose from prejudice.

He stayed with a friend until the house was sold, accepted the position in Miami, and moved to an apartment in Coral Gables, not far from where he had lived before with Brad. Two years later when the owners sold the building to a South American businessman who wanted to almost double his rent, he moved down the street to the apartment on the side of the flamingo house on Sidonia Avenue.

When he first moved in, the place was little more than a garage with a bathroom, a kitchen, and a front door. The terrazzo floors were damaged beyond repair and the cabinets above the sink were painted dark blue. Its dinginess was a sharp contrast to the grandeur of the rest of the house. John overhauled the room, sealed up the holes in the screens, laid down a carpet, mirrored one wall and created a bedroom area that was concealed from the front part of the room. There was even a space for his sit-up bench. He had turned his garage into a livable sanctuary—a needed retreat. When the landlady saw it, she couldn't stop talking. She was glad he was there. As she put it, "It was nice to have a man around." He only hoped that she wasn't pleased enough to raise the rent.

The knock at the door came at the appropriate hour. Bob came in, and because of the low ceiling, looked even taller than John remembered.

"Oh, this is nice," he said, looking with interest around the apartment. "Very homey, sort of cozy."

"Thank you. Every space is functional."

"I can see that. I almost went to the main house, but then I remember you said it was on the side. Your landlady would have thought she was getting company."

"She'd probably have invited you in for tea."

"I'm sorry that I called so late. That wasn't much notice, I know."

"Oh that's all right," John brushed it off and tried to act casual. "I'm glad you did. I was hoping to hear from you."

"Well, I'd been thinking about you. I've just been so busy getting this new program set up at the clinic, and then the groups meet on Monday and Wednesday nights so . . . but I'm glad we finally got to get together again."

"Me too," John said, wondering whether to ask Bob to sit down and talk for awhile or to suggest leaving for the restaurant. Those opening moments were always awkward.

Carlos made it look so easy. He seemed to have a knack for entertaining that John envied, especially at times like these.

Bob resolved the dilemma by sitting down on his own, and John moved next to him on the sofa. "I think I was being a little bold there at Carlos' when I gave you my number."

"Well," Bob said, "if you didn't, I was going to give you mine."

"That's a relief."

Bob's eyes darted around the room. "How long have you lived here?"

"About a year and a half I guess. I was only going to stay a few months and then get a bigger place, but it was so affordable that it seemed foolish to give it up, even though it wasn't exactly what I needed."

"Well, you've made it very comfortable," Bob said. "You're going to have to pick the place for tonight because I don't know too much about this end of town."

"All right, I know a little place we can go. Are you ready?"

"Yeah," Bob got up. John turned out the light and followed him out the front door. The car was parked at the curb. He unlocked the passenger door and pulled it open, ran around to the other side, brushed the violet orchid petals off the roof, opened his own door, and climbed in.

The Coconut Grove Hotel was a tall, thin building with a square base that rose up out of blankets of green palm fronds. John parked the car on Darwin Road. They walked up the curving stone driveway that constituted one of the very few hills in South Florida. A clump of giant Banyan trees stood in a semi-circle between the driveway and the street, branching out over their heads like an umbrella protecting the entrance. The car attendant called a familiar hello to John as they ascended the steps to the main lobby. The Café Brasserie was off to the left. A middle-aged maitré d' with a bald spot gave them a table for two overlooking the pool and seated them next to each other. A young waitress with an English accent took their order and returned shortly with two glasses of white wine. John's deep brown eyes sparkled in the candlelight, his face softly aglow. Bob looked at him, settling finally on his eyes and raised his wine glass. "Here's to new friends."

"To new friends." They clinked.

"So, how long have you lived in Miami," John asked, feeling the warmth of the wine in his stomach.

"About a year. I moved down from Pennsylvania because I got tired of shoveling snow."

"Where in Pennsylvania?"

"Lancaster."

"You're kidding. I lived in Lancaster for about six months," John said wondering what it might have been like to live in the rolling Pennsylvania countryside with this man.

"Oh, then you must have gone to the Tally-Ho."

"Yes," John sounded astonished.

"I can't believe all this. In the car, coming over I find out that your birthday is on the same day as mine but a year later, then I find out we lived in the same town. . . ."

"To old neighbors," John smiled and raised his glass.

"To old neighbors," they clinked again.

Bob spoke easily. In the several hours they spent together, they got to know one another more intimately than they knew many of the people with whom they worked every day. In this short amount of time, they allowed themselves the vulnerability of sharing.

The check came and John reached for his wallet, but Bob claimed the ticket, saying that he had extended the invitation. John was warmed by the gesture and wondered if it meant that this man was displaying a special interest in him. Somehow, in a convoluted way, the check became synonymous with romantic interest—a kind of throwback to traditional romantic straight relationships where the gentleman took his date out to dinner. If they went dutch, it implied that they were just friends, but if the man paid, he wanted more than a pat on the back. John tried to keep things in perspective and not let himself get too carried away by remembering that Bob probably made four times his salary and a dinner didn't put much of a dent in his budget. He remembered the story of the Count and the pauper, each of whom donated a dollar to the coffers of the temple. To the Count it meant nothing more than a showy gesture, but to the pauper it was everything.

When they got back to John's apartment, he poured two glasses of wine and they sat on the couch. By this time they were both relaxed and content, the kind of contentment that comes with the anticipation of good things. Bob slipped off his loafers and on his host's recommendation, lifted his feet up onto the sofa. John stroked them gently as they talked. He slipped his hand up under Bob's trouser and felt the hair on his legs. Soon he found himself lying head to chest against this golden apparition. He felt like a lodestar pulling on a passing meteor that had come too close. John was unsure of his actions and didn't know how to initiate further intimacy without appearing brazen. He didn't want Bob to think that he was crude, yet all of his thoughts were focused on the physical.

"Would you like to stay with me tonight?"

"I'm not sure. I should probably be heading back."

"I wish you didn't have to go. I feels so good to be next to you."

"Mmm. You too. You're nice."

They held each other for what seemed like a long time and talked about how wonderful they felt. John ached to please him.

"I've got a decision to make here, don't I?" Bob said heavily as though some serious judgement rested upon his choice to stay.

John, sensing his anguish, gave him a friendly kiss on the cheek and said, "No, I know. You have to be getting back. Maybe another time."

"I want to be able to spend the whole night with you."

A shiver went down John's spine. He had thought for a moment that Bob was not interested in him, but this one sentence set everything right. He felt good. Actually, he didn't mind giving Bob up. He was satisfied with simply touching him—a rare occurrence. He knew somewhere deep within him that this man was different. There was no resentment in their parting. They said good night with a lingering kiss, Bob's large hand on the back of John's head. As he closed the door, John was filled with a sense of well being. As he undressed, he reviewed all that had been said and relived the evening a hundred times. He shut out the light, climbed into bed, and relived it a hundred more.

On the same night that John had been exalted by love Matthew was sitting in his living room watching television. Johnny Carson had just introduced his last guest when Larry walked in.

"Well, it's about time you got home."

"Yeah, well I had to meet somebody after work."

"No call or anything?"

"I didn't think of it."

Matthew was maddened by the casual statement. "That's all you can say, 'I didn't think of it?'"

"Look, Matthew. I'm in no mood to argue."

"I would have appreciated it if you would tell me, so I know not to make dinner for you."

"We're not married any more. You don't have to wait up for me or cook my dinner."

"Oh, well thanks for telling me. From now on cook your own damn meals, or better yet, have Walter do it for you. That's who you were with, wasn't it?"

"Just leave me alone."

"As soon as you answer my question. You were with Walter again, weren't you?"

"Yes, God damn it. What else you want to know? Did we have sex? Yes, we did. What else?"

"Oh, I figured that."

"Then what are you asking me for?"

"I wanted to hear it from you."

"What do you want me to do, Matthew? You want me to stop going out? Is that it?"

"No. I just want you to think about me once in a while. I'm not asking you to stop going out. Just let me know. I cooked dinner for you tonight." He buckled and started to sob.

Larry came over and put his arm around Matthew. "All right, all right. Look, I'm sorry. I'm just tired that's all. Walter was giving me a hard time; then I come home and you're giving me a hard time. I didn't mean to yell."

"I feel like an idiot doing things for you sometimes. I made a special trip to the store to get fresh onions and lettuce, and then you didn't even come home. You were out with that guy again. Are you two getting serious?" he pulled away from Larry.

"C'mon, Matthew."

"I'd like to know. If you tell me the truth, I can deal with it. It's not knowing what's going on that gives me problems. Just be honest with me, that's all."

"It's regular. I don't know if that's serious."

"Do you love him?"

"I don't know."

"You don't know," Matthew repeated somberly.

"No, I don't."

The Carson theme song rang out and the credits quickly crossed the screen. Matthew clicked the set off, walked into his own room, and closed the door.

6.

It was late June, just after the summer solstice, and according to Carlos, the Ladies' Auxiliary was about to meet. Tonight would be special: a dress-up dinner at the Esplanade in the Hyatt Regency. No dates, no boyfriends, just the three of them getting together for a good time. They met at Carlos' townhouse. John wore his blue suit and red silk tie. Matthew decided on a preppy tan corduroy coat with patches on the elbows, brown slacks, and penny loafers. Carlos had a white dinner jacket and black pants.

Just before they were about to leave for downtown, Carlos decided to show his friends the wig he had bought for an upcoming party. It was long, brown, and curly. Watching himself in the mirror behind the dining room table, he pulled the wig over his head. Then, primping, he said, "What do you think?"

"It looks so . . . temporary," Matthew said.

"Well," Carlos responded, putting each curl in place, "You know the old saying, 'Hair today, gone tomorrow!'"

"I didn't hair you," Matthew said.

"Hair we go again," Carlos said.

"Seen any good-looking tortoises lately?" John said.

"What?" both said.

Matthew frowned. "I should have brought my polaroid. We could frame you and put you on the bureau next to mom and dad."

"Yes," John said. "Can't you see them showing off the family photos . . . 'and this is our son, Carlos. He's a little strange.'"

"More than a little, I'm afraid," Matthew said gravely.

"Eccentric, dear. All great minds are slightly eccentric." Carlos continued to look at himself in the large mirror. "There's something distinguished about the hair when you look at it with the dinner jacket."

"Distinguished?" Matthew mused. "I would have said disgusting."

"Now wait a minute," John intervened. "I think he's got something."

"Don't you think I look like a movie star, Matthew?"

"Yes, E. T."

"Now look at me objectively," Carlos said, "as if you didn't know me."

"Oh, what a lovely thought," Matthew jested.

"Actually, I rather look like a gifted concert pianist on tour," he said rather grandly.

"Well, then," Matthew countered, "I think you should wear it to dinner just to demonstrate your strength of conviction."

"I wouldn't go that far." Carlos beat a hasty retreat.

"Why not?" John said. "You really do look good in it."

"Distinguished," Matthew reminded.

"You really think so?" Carlos thought of the possibilities.

"You could be traveling incognito," John urged. "We'll cover for you."

"Well, I don't know."

"Oh, come on. You look terrific," Matthew said. "Besides, our reservation is for eight o'clock."

"Why not?" Carlos said, grabbing a pair of sunglasses. "They do need someone to look up to." And out into the thick night they went, walking right past the old lady next door who was coming home and didn't recognize Carlos.

Matthew took them in his small gray station wagon. Completely without glamour, it had plastic wood molding and a rack on top. "One of these days I'm going to get a car that's a little more gay."

"You mean a Volkswagen?" Carlos said.

"He means something sporty," John said.

"Yeah. This was okay for what I was doing, but now I want something different."

They picked up the expressway at Vizcaya and watched the single family houses being replaced by huge condominium complexes. It was only a short run until the car turned off the ramp that set them down at the base of the skyscrapers downtown. Matthew carefully circumnavigated the temporary yellow barricades (something was always being dug up or constructed) and turned up the steep curving incline that led to the entrance of the hotel. They stopped under the canopy. A young man barely out of college opened the passenger door, and Carlos emerged, followed by John. Matthew opened the driver's door himself and headed around the front. With an inner chuckle, he waited for the attendant's reaction.

"Good evening," Carlos said to the boy.

"Evening, sir," the young man replied and then walked around, as usual, to the front of the car and handed Matthew a ticket. Carlos could hardly control his excitement. They might just pull this caper off. The three young men, one a gifted celebrity, strolled into the lobby. Two young girls passed by and looked Carlos up and down. Except for the gleam in his eye, he gave no indication that he had noticed their interest. He was just another supremely confident and aloof young man out for an evening of fun.

They entered the restaurant and asked for the small room which was more intimate. The host seated them without a glimmer of surprise, as though he came across men with long flowing locks every other day. The waiters gathered and drew straws to see which one of them would get table three.

"This is nice. I'm glad we decided to come," Matthew said.

"Nice but dark," Carlos countered. "I can't even see what I'm ordering, though I'm sure it's expensive."

"Take off the sunglasses," John said and shot Matthew an unbelieving glance.

"Oh, that's much better," Carlos said, putting on his usual round glasses with the Scarlett frames. "I'm so glad the table cloths aren't really purple. There's something terribly disturbing about purple, don't you think? You'd never see a real man wearing it. But then who knows about such things? Certainly no one at this table."

John ignored him, as he usually did whenever Carlos threatened to dissolve the ambiguous line between masculine and feminine. Carlos, aware of John's sensitivity to the subject, took advantage of every opportunity to raise the issue. After all, it was for John's own good; what nobler reason could there be? Matthew, on the other hand, found it all too amusing. Both of them felt that Carlos' abandon made even the dreariest aspects of life palatable. Wars and rumors of wars appeared in the Sunday Herald, and Carlos was perturbed by none of them. Matthew was incensed by what he read, but realized that there was nothing he could do. John had stopped reading the paper altogether. In general, what he could not face, he ignored. Neither understood how Carlos went through life without worrying, but they were glad that he did. Carlos was glib, unaffected, and possessed the quality of detachment that John, especially, coveted.

The waiter greeted them and took their orders for appetizers. As John spooned up his vichyssoise, he said, "Did you ever notice how we do everything at the dinner table with only one hand?"

"There are only so many things one can do at a dinner table in public," Carlos responded. "What would you like to be doing with your other hand?"

"Be nice, Carlos," Matthew cut in. "I don't think he's used to your brand of humor yet."

"What was I going to say?"

"I don't think you were going to suggest that he work on his taxes."

"Well, read my rights! No wonder Larry doesn't like you any more."

"He's got a new boyfriend now," Matthew said seemingly unaffected by Carlos' barb.

"That must be really tough on you," John commented.

"Not anymore. You can get used to anything."

"I wish you'd find an apartment of your own," John said.

"You need to be in the South End with us," Carlos said. "There's nothing worthwhile north of downtown other than Karleman's on a Saturday night."

"I've been living in that house for ten years. I don't know what it would be like to have my own place." Matthew had bought the house with Larry at a fraction of the cost for which they could sell it. He could still remember the evening after they had moved in when the two of them were sitting around the living room deciding how to arrange it. Larry had said, "I don't care what you do on the inside, but in the yard I want to see palm trees. If we're living in Florida we have to have palm trees." So the next day Larry went out and bought four different kinds of palms, none of which were indigenous to the area. When he planted them in a row across the front of the house, they didn't live up to the image he had of them. They looked small, skinny and isolated, not at all like the postcards he'd seen, so he went out and bought nine more. He watered the slow growing sticks every day without fail and cared for them like children sprung from his own seed. But after the first year he became weary and figured they would manage on their own, not realizing that, unlike human beings, their first five years of life were the slowest. Though sparse in their infancy, the trees blossomed unexpectedly into a massive grove—so thick and close together that the house was almost hidden behind them. They finally looked like the postcards, and Larry had sent pictures of them to his mother in Queens. Matthew could remember as though it were only last week— the palms, the new house, the feelings.

The skinny, light–haired waiter came back to clean the table. When he returned with the entrées, he didn't ask who ordered what but laid down the correct plate before each of them, smiling as he did so. Carlos watched until he caught the waiter's eye and said, "What is your name?"

"Hans," the young man said politely.

"Hans," Carlos repeated. "What a charming name. From the people who brought us the master race, I believe. Are you German?"

"Yes."

"I could tell by the hair and the eyes. You know who I am, of course."

"No. I'm sorry." the waiter said shyly.

"Carlos Montana. But please keep it to yourself. At least until we leave. I really don't want people to know."

"The name sounds familiar," he lied, standing next to the table.

"The concert pianist. I'm in your lovely town for two glorious nights and then it's back to the airways. Oh, I hate it. I'd love to just settle down in one place, but such is life. You're doing a fine job, by the way."

"Thank you, sir. I hope you enjoy your meal. Call me if you need me." Discreetly, he left them alone in the small room.

"The age of innocence," Carlos said to the others.

"We tend to admire what we don't have," Matthew said.

"So what's new with Randy?" John asked, looking at Carlos.

"Oh, my God," Matthew said and turned to Carlos. "Didn't you tell him about the other night?" and proceeded to reveal how he had been "maliciously" stashed in a closet and how close they had come to "death" that night.

"I thought he'd never leave," Carlos punctuated. "I was scared shitless."

"YOU were scared?" Matthew exclaimed. "I was the one standing on your dirty linen. I still get the shivers thinking what would have happened if he opened the door instead of you."

"Oh, you worry too much."

"Well, what happened after you left? I still haven't heard that story," Matthew said.

"We talked and worked through some things. Like, I told him what I was feeling and he told me what he was feeling. I wanted to know what was going on with him. I told him that I was mad, but I couldn't be too mad because he was even madder at me that night. Pent-up hostility. I had no idea."

"Well, good," Matthew said. "At least you're bringing it all out into the open and not letting it build up inside."

"Oh, yes, I felt it was important to let him know, and like I said, we talked. I guess we just want different things."

"What do you mean?"

"I told him I didn't like the idea of him going out with other guys. He thinks I'm being childish. Do you think I'm being childish?"

"No," Matthew answered. "I don't think it's childish to let your intentions be known, but if you do that, you have to be able to accept the possibility that he may not want the same thing. And from what I could hear, he knew that you were fooling around too."

"Of course he did. I'm not going to sit home and knit while he goes out a-whoring. Goose and gander and all that stuff. Although I must say, I do knit a mean afghan."

"Are you going to see him again?" John prodded.

"No."

"You aren't?" Matthew sounded surprised.

"No, dear. I've finally come to my senses. I don't want a lover. I want to be free and unencumbered, to roam as I please like the beasts of the Serengeti."

The conflicting notions of monogamy and freedom each sounded wonderful under the magical spell of Carlos' imagery. The attributes of whichever one he was in agreement with at the time was magnified and made beautiful. But the two ideals were opposite extremes, neither one approaching moderation. How could he fluctuate so easily from one end of the spectrum to the other?

During desert, Matthew said, "Vic Ramona called me again Wednesday night and wanted to go out."

"Did you tell him no again?" Carlos asked.

"Of course. He's such an earthman."

"Oh?" Carlos arched his right brow.

"He has this irritating need to be macho and pushy and besides, I'm not into all that hair."

"I am," Carlos said.

"You know, it was Ramona who told me what a hairy man hates more than anything else in the world."

"What's that," Carlos asked, shoveling his chocolate mousse.

"Soft toilet paper."

Carlos choked on the mousse. "Really! Would cardboard stand up to the pressure?"

Hans, the young waiter, looked at the three laughing hysterically, as he brought three cups and a silver pot of coffee. He set them down and poured, then left the pot there.

"Maybe you should give Vic's number to Carlos, now that he's free again," John said.

"I'm through with love," Carlos lamented.

"I don't know. I think there is something to be said for loving," John reflected as he poured cream into his cup. "At least I hope there is."

"Oh, yes, we musn't dash his hopes," Matthew said.

Then turning to John, he asked, "How is this flaming romance going with Bob?"

"It's going great. We went to an exhibit at the Metropolitan downtown and he bought me a poster as sort of a commemoration of the evening. I really like him a lot," he raised the cup to his lips.

"I thought you've been grinning a little too much lately," Carlos said.

"We have things in common. I almost can't believe it's true."

"Oh God. Pass the sugar," Carlos said seriously, looking out over the top of his glasses.

"And little incidents happen, you know, where you both discover that you like the same crazy things that no one else likes," John said, passing the sugar to Carlos.

"Stage one."

"What?"

"Randy and I did the same thing. It was wonderful at first."

"Come on, Carlos. I really feel good about this."

"I'm not saying you shouldn't feel good about it. I'm just telling you not to put all of your hopes on this thing."

"I think I already am."

"But you don't have any commitments, right?" Matthew cleared.

"No," John answered

"You're just dating now," Matthew commanded rather than asked.

"Right."

"No problem there," Matthew said to Carlos.

"I didn't say there was a problem," Carlos defended his position. "He simply said that he's put a lot of hopes on this affair."

"I guess what I meant was that I'm enjoying it," John said.

"Oh. Okay. I thought you were already getting involved."

John opened his mouth to answer but decided against it. Instead, he thought, quietly to himself. "Just because it didn't work out between you and Randy, doesn't mean it can't work out between Bob and me."

"Can I get you anything else, gentlemen?"

"Well . . ." Carlos droned, twisting a long curl around his finger.

"That's all, thank you," Matthew intervened.

7.

This time John was looking for something more in a lover, a partner whose interests extended beyond sex. He had studied philosophy and comparative religions and wanted someone with whom he could relate to on an intellectual as well as a physical plane. He wanted to explore esoteric thought and ponder metaphysical ideas and he just couldn't do that, he realized, in a discotheque. But he went to the discos faithfully each weekend, like a monk to chapel, praying for deliverance.

He was fascinated by the Dead Sea Scrolls and often sat rereading the accounts and records of their authors, the Essenes. They were a mystical sect of Judaism who were called fanatics and sorcerers by their enemies. Their very name was a Roman slur meaning "expectant ones" and possibly from their ranks the Messiah had made his appearance at the expected time. John felt a certain amount of kinship with them in their persecution. Like his own community, they were not well received by the people of their time. Yet from their ranks emerged greatness, and he took comfort in that.

He had great expectations in Bob, who seemed to be unlike the other men who had filtered through his life. They had been seeing each other regularly (always at John's apartment), and the crowd at the 500 Club already talked about them as a pair. John enjoyed their conclusions but neither encouraged nor denied them.

"One of these days," Charles had said to him, "we'd like to have you and Bob over for dinner."

"Oh, that would be nice." John said.

"Not this weekend because we're going up to Palm Beach to see Mike's parents but how about the Saturday after?"

"I'll have to see what Bob's schedule is," he glowed.

"Good, just give a call sometime during the week. We're both in the book."

John called Bob the next night to tell him. "By the way, Mike and Charles asked if we'd have dinner at their place next weekend."

"They asked you?"

"Yes, I went to a Wednesday niter. I said I'd check with you."

"I think I've got a seminar then. It'd probably be better if we made it for some other time."

"Fine. I'll let them know."

"I've known Charles for years. I can't believe he didn't ask me."

"You weren't there, obviously."

"Oblivously. Do you know that he's started asking me how you are?"

"Just smile and tell him I'm fine."

"You're fine," Bob repeated, as in a stupor.

"Perfect," John said.

Bob was in every sense of the word, a humanist, at least as far as John could see. He had been offered a cushy position in the North End catering to a wealthy clientel with anxiety syndromes, but turned it down to work at Jackson Memorial Hospital with people who really needed him. He gave up the Mercedes for a Toyota. He followed his own path and hadn't yet succumbed to the great god of finance. He even went to church on Sundays, which attracted John to him all the more.

John was never considered traditional in his own beliefs, choosing to acknowledge the continuity of life rather than the idea of heaven and hell as places to which one ultimately travels like going to Monaco. He thought of them as more a part of life than death, that people he passed on the street or worked with at the office were already in one place or the other or someplace in between. He considered the possibility of having known Bob in some remote past life, given the intensity of attraction which had been in force since the beginning.

Ordinarily, John was in complete control of any relationship. But this—this was something beyond him. He felt that a bond was being established between them that was more than glandular, although, to be fair, he would not complain if it never amounted to more than that.

Bob was attractive but he was not the type to rush into sex. John remembered their first evening together. They had consummated their "friendship" the second time around. If John listed all of the things in a man that he found stimulating, he would describe Bob. He was surprised to learn in talking of his feelings, that Matthew and Carlos did not react in a similar manner, but to him, Bob's deep blue eyes seemed hypnotic. John told his friends that Bob reminded him of the character who had appeared repeatedly in his dreams of the preceding year. The dream figure came forward in different circumstances but he always was the same person: a tall, blonde, and slender man. They rendezvoused on another plane, another level of consciousness. But who was this guardian phantom? Matthew's explanation was that the mystery man was the projection of an ideal image—and that may have been true— but, John insisted, he looked exactly like Bob.

"Listen, dear," Carlos told him, putting an arm around John's shoulder. "Quite frankly, I wouldn't tell that story to too many people."

"I don't."

"That's good. You see, the trouble with you, John, is that you're a dreamer. You're living in a stained glass window, like John the Beloved. You've got to tough up a little."

"YOU'RE telling ME to tough up?"

"Listen, I may be small, but I know what's going on. Nobody takes advantage of me."

"Nobody is taking advantage of anybody, and besides, I don't know if I want to toughen up. I'm an artist."

"Well . . . I suppose one must weigh the alternatives."

It was ironic. John had found a man with whom he could consider the possibility of a long-term relationship. Bob was thoughtful but self-protective, loving but careful, sexual but spiritual. In short, he was very much like John. He often used to wonder whether it was better to love someone just like himself or to love someone completely different. At least with a man of similar ways and means, they could share their interest and celebrate the joys of life. But John's reaction was one of apprehension rather than joy.

He remembered what had happened the last time he allowed himself to become emotionally involved, more than two years ago. He had become obsessed with a man who had sent him conflicting signals, and John, who accepted everything at face value, had a hard time dealing with the ambiguity. Moreover, it came at a time when so many other changes were taking place in his life. One evening his world came apart—the night they had taken acid with speed. Toward the end of the night, John had become overly sentimental and whimpered, "I feel so close to you."

The man responded with, "John, you have to learn to control your emotions."

And then came that terrible fear. The panic and the paranoia that lasted through the night and were gone by morning. But the relationship continued to be destructive.

John took whatever he could until a few months later when, in the midst of anger, the terrible fear which he had experienced the night they took the drugs inexplicably snapped back into force and did not diminish in its intensity for months. During that nightmarish period, his hands trembled and his heart raced. He woke up afraid and went to bed afraid. He couldn't get on a crowded bus and panicked at the thought of using the elevator at the office. He ended the relationship, unable to function socially, but the trauma remained, and he generalized his experience to include all relationships.

For two years he had avoided any hint of intimacy and steered clear of love's bondage. He could show interest in people without feeling threatened, but involvement was much too risky. That was why it was so much easier to become involved with people who loved him rather than those he loved. He did not want to lose control again the way he did before. The feeling of panic that he associated with that relationship kept him at arm's length. And now for the first time since then, John found himself becoming involved with another man. Would the same thing happen again? Would that awful helplessness return? He couldn't bear that again. He wouldn't bear that again.

But how was he to unlearn an emotional reaction? How could he reconcile love and fear? He'd have to relive the experience again, only this time the result must be good. That's where the risk was—in the ending. He fantasized what the ending would be like with Bob even before the beginning. Would it be good, indifferent, or catastrophic?

The next time he was to see Bob, he had spent part of the day repeating to himself, "This is not the same thing. This is not the same thing. Everything will be fine." He'd said it over and over again, until finally the words sank down deep into his sub-conscious, and the fear left him. Matthew had told him that it was not the relationship that caused him to break down, it was his own thoughts that did it. He did not have to react with resentment. He might have accepted the circumstances as they were without wishing to change what could not be changed. He might have allowed his lover to be himself and simply adjusted to the situation or withdrawn quietly. Instead, he had become enraged, and since his friend was above reproach, had kept it within himself. There was an invaluable lesson in that experience. He did not have to let it happen again. He told himself that, no matter what happened this time, he would let Bob be Bob, accepting the cards as they were dealt.

Without realizing it, he was saying yes again. In the deeper recesses of his mind, he was opening up once more. He was daring to risk again. A subtle change was taking place, a change that he could feel but did not accept, and it was this unconscious opening that riddled him with terror, and filled him with an inexplicable uneasiness. A movement was taking place in the uncharted depths of his consciousness and all because of this blue-eyed phantom.

He thought about all these things as he drove along I-95. The lines in the road whizzed by, the wind gushed through the open window, and fluttered his hair. The car seemed to be operating on its own cognizance, as if it knew exactly which turns to make and what lane to be in without its driver giving it a thought. The sign for 151st Street finally came into view, and John turned east into Biscayne Gardens and looked for the trees and landmarks that according to the directions he had received, told him that he was approaching Bob's house.

He pulled the green Triumph into the driveway. The house looked deserted except for the open front door, which was protected by a deco screen door that allowed the breeze to pass through. It was held together by a life-sized aluminum flamingo with radiating spokes that touched the frame around its upper half. A clump of palm fronds hung over the entrance like a giant umbrella shielding and protecting it from the sun and rain. The base of the tree was hidden in a cluster of

Salome that grew on the ground and threw out fanlike leaves to shade the life giving properties of the soil below, already bleached and laid barren by the Florida sun. The lawn was clipped like all of the other lawns in the upper-middle-class residential neighborhood.

John climbed out of the car, walked up to the door, and rang the bell. He looked up at a clump of coconuts hanging on the tree beside him, and wondered how much longer it would be before they grew directly over the doorway. Would Bob cut the tree down then to prevent a possible law suit, or just keep collecting the heavy fruit? Did he even think about it?

"Hi," called a voice from the darkness within. The screen door opened.

"Hello," John waited until the door closed and then put his arms around Bob's neck.

"Mmmm. It's good to see you," Bob responded to the affection.

"You too," John said.

"Have any trouble finding it?"

"Not a bit. I have an excellent sense of direction."

"Good. Come on in," Bob said, walking through to the room in the back. "Can I get you something to drink. I know you don't like alcohol, but I have coke."

"Caffeine."

"Seven-up or lemonade?"

"Lemonade sounds good," John said, sitting down in a rattan chair with a deep green cushion that needed to be replaced.

"Okay." Bob went off in search of lemonade.

"This is a beautiful house."

"Thank you," Bob said from the kitchen. "I'm not sure I'm going to stay though."

"Why's that?"

"Oh, I don't know. It's big and I really don't need all of this."

"Must be a lot to clean. I have enough of a problem with my place, which is as big as your Florida room."

"Right." He handed John his glass and sat down. "I thought about getting a roommate but I may just sell it and get it off my hands."

"It might be easier, I guess," John said, not really knowing what he was talking about.

"And cheaper. Half my salary goes into the mortgage for this place. The other half goes into keeping it up. Anything left over I get to spend on the groceries."

"What is it, two bedrooms?"

"Yes, I'll show you." He gave John the tour.

"Why do you sleep in the smaller bedroom?" John was looking at the king-sized bed. "Most people would take the larger."

"Well," Bob said slowly, "it's quieter back here. Front room faces the street."

"That's true." They moved back to the Florida room.

"How are Carlos and Matthew doing?" Bob said to change the subject. "Have you seen them lately?"

"Oh, yes. We took Matthew out to dinner for his birthday. They were asking about you."

"I hope you told them something good."

"Are you kidding?" John wanted to go over, sit down close to Bob, touch him, and feel him. But he restrained himself. The time would come later.

Bob was talking about his day at the hospital, and John found himself being drawn into his friend's life. He was becoming familiar with the people with whom Bob worked and with his daily routine. They were like characters in a story. Bob had said he wanted him to meet them someday. He wondered what Bob had said to them about his current affair. Did he speak with affection or annoyance?

The phone rang and Bob picked it up. He seemed glad to hear from the other party and had no reservations about talking in front of his guest. John would have felt stifled if the situation were reversed, and he had gotten the call. He was much more private, almost secretive. He went to the bathroom to allow Bob a little more privacy. His urine was yellow from the Vitamin B capsule that he had taken earlier, and it mixed with the Tidy blue water in the bowl to create a deep green pool. It reminded him of the colored water in the fancy bottles at the pharmacy counter where he filled his prescriptions. He thought of how the mixture in the bowl would look in one of those bottles and imagined little old ladies coming into the store from confession and admiring the color if his urine. He flushed, ran water over his hands, and walked out. Bob was still on the phone, so he wandered about the living room. There was a photo on the mantle over the fireplace, blown up and cropped so that it only showed from the shoulders up, leaving you to guess what the other half was like. A young man, in an open shirt looking somber, stood in front of a mud hut. It was framed very simply and leaned on a trangular felt piece that lifted off the backing.

He heard Bob getting ready to hang up and meandered back toward the Florida room. "I'm sorry," Bob said. "That was a friend of mine who I haven't heard from in months."

They finished their drinks and had three more before deciding that they didn't want to see a movie. Bob had communicated his desire for affection through touch, and John responded by bravely saying, "Shall I stay over tonight?"

"I just took it for granted that you would," Bob said.

"Oh, things are looking up. Let me go to my car and get my things."

"Glad to see that you came prepared."

"I always hope for the best."

"Go get your things," Bob said, giving John a pat on the rear.

While John was at the car, Bob dimmed the lights in the

back of the house. When he heard the front door shut, he yelled, "Lock it."

"All right," John said, and came back, dropping his overnight bag near the bedroom door. He noticed the change in the room and sat on the sofa again next to Bob. An arm wrapped around John's neck as he sat back and sighed with relief. "This is nice. I love soft lights."

"Atmosphere."

"If I had the choice of going out to eat at a place that had terrific food but poor surroundings or a place that had atmosphere and mediocre food, I think I'd choose the atmosphere."

"If they're smart, they'll have both."

"Hypothetically, I mean. When I go out, part of the excitement is in knowing that I'm in a place which is extraordinary. I can make good food at home."

"Oh, really," Bob said, taking one of John's hands and caressing each finger. "I'll have to get you to make dinner for me some night."

"I'd like to do that. I'll even furnish the Alka-Seltzer."

He laughed, "You're too modest."

"I'd reserve judgement for awhile."

"You know you have beautiful hands," Bob said running his lips along each finger. "Expressive and long." John felt attractive, desirable. "Piano fingers, they used to call them."

"I used to play the piano," John added trying to keep his composure.

"Used to?"

"I had to sell it. Such a beautiful piece too. Upright, molded legs. They don't make them that way anymore."

"Did you take lessons?"

"I have to confess," John said. "Like all good Italian boys, I took lessons on the accordion."

"No kidding."

"Don't you go telling anyone."

"I think that's great." Bob smiled.

"That's two of you, including my professori. I studied for nine years at the conservatory in Hollywood."

"Florida."

"Florida. But then I grew up and I . . ."

"Did you?" Bob interrupted.

"Did I what?"

"Grow up."

"Oh, get smart," John said, pushing Bob's face gently away as he laughed. "Yes, I did grow up and decided that I wanted to play the piano. So I traded in the accordion. Actually, I bought it for my lover. I had a lover for five years. And he already played, but we didn't have a piano so it was perfect."

"Must have been easy for you to pick up," Bob said, keeping the conversation light. "Same keyboard and all."

"The right hand was great. The left hand was spastic. If they could only tilt the thing on its side, I'd have played even better."

"Creature of habit," Bob condescended.

"Aren't we all?" John countered.

"Are you saying I'm a creature of habit?"

"A very cute creature."

Bob moaned. "You know just what to say don't you?" He moved in closer and kissed John.

"I must be doing something right," John murmured. He opened one of Bob's shirt buttons and put his hand inside to stroke the hair on his chest while they kissed.

"Let's go inside."

8.

The weeks flew by and summer became more intense. A wealthy friend of John's had once told him that the only people who stayed in Miami during the summer were those who had to. John conceded and said that the summers in Florida were just as miserable as the winters in New York. But he was one of the many who stayed in Miami that summer, along with Matthew and Carlos and all of the others who worked for a living.

The weekend came, as it always did, to relieve them of the dreary hours they spent bound to an office or to a drawing table, trying to make their bosses look good. And like all other weekends, an appearance at Karleman's, or some other place like it, was considered necessary. It was almost an obligation forced upon them by the pressures of time, for to miss the gathering this weekend might mean another seven days before the opportunity of a chance transformation of their lives would present itself again. John had given up those late nights during the week when he would sneak into bed at 3:00 A.M. and get up again at 6:30. He wanted to be as stable and practical as Matthew. Though Matthew thought nothing of going out during the week, he had the restraint and force of will to leave by 1:00 A.M. John had difficulty showing moderation in anything. It was better for him not to have something at all than to have it in limited portions. Everything in Miami started so late. He wondered how anyone here could work and still do the things they did. But the latenight, weekday crowd consisted of waiters, hotel personnel, actors, flight attendants—the people who didn't share a nine-to-five existence, and the wealthy who didn't work at all.

John set up the ironing board, pressed the polo shirt he bought with no emblem so that he wouldn't be like everybody else, and hung his tight, faded jeans out on the chin-up bar that stretched across the bathroom doorjamb. He reached in behind the plastic, see-through curtain and turned on the hot water for his second shower of the day. No matter how clean he was, he always took a shower before going to the bars. America was obsessed with odor. Television was cashing in with messages that told how to keep smelling sweet and peddled anything from shoe ventilators to jock spray; from breath mints to feminine deodorants. The most devastating thought was the possibility of meeting someone interesting— someone to impress—and bringing him home to find that bacteria had multiplied on your private parts. He remembered how the tour guide at the Vizcaya Mansion told the group that the French survived formal parties, before they learned how to paralyze sweat glands, by creating fabulous candle chandeliers with metal cups filled with perfume that sat above each flame. As the liquid heated it would fill the room with its scent and mix with the odor of musky armpits and damp torsos.

Carlos would say, "I don't see how any gay man survived before the advent of Bloomingdale's."

John would say, "I could survive anything as long as I had love."

And Matthew would say, "We'd deal with it. After all, what do you think the next century is going to say about us?"

John sneaked out the front door past the landlady's window, where she sat like a sentry reading her Bible, and headed for Karleman's. It was a small, intimate bar that converted into a discotheque on the weekends. One long room with paintings on the wall, it had a horseshoe bar at one end and a dance floor at the other. It was friendly and more conservative than the cavernous bars of downtown or the warehouse district where one had to get used to the idea of being jostled and pushed by young boys who acted as though they 'just got off the boat.' And in some cases they just did. Carlos had a Cuban friend whose sole purpose was to meet newly arriving homosexual refugees and introduce them to the open spectacle of the American Gay Discotheque. A guide, of sorts, leading his everchanging entourage through the Elysian fields where they saw men unashamed to dance with one another. There was no such place in Cuba, where known homosexuals were reduced to cleaning the streets.

Karleman's was the official meeting place of the Ladies' Auxiliary. The smoke-filled room glowed in an other-worldly light as bodies huddled shoulder to shoulder. Instinctive migrations began and ended with every record change that exploded from the turntables of the disc jockey's perch. He sat above the crowd like Thor, hurling down, not lightning bolts, but the ever-more persuasive power of the explosive music. Janet had once asked, "Why doesn't the gay community, which is so prevalent in the music industry, put out more music with positive gay messages. It could turn the tide of opinion."

"I don't know," John had answered, "maybe they're afraid."

Tonight, as always, people danced in a daze with eyes lifted up toward heaven, sedated by the rhythmic wave that consumed their bodies like one giant heartbeat. Together they moved with illusory partners, for they really danced with everyone on the floor. It was possible to transfer your attention so that you were, in effect, dancing with the person next to you or with the person across the floor, whom you had admired earlier. And both would be aware of the intimate union that was taking place, though it might never be acknowledged. Every body moved in unison like drops of water in an advancing wave. Each, a part of the whole, swaying and undulating according to a precise formula emanating from the huge carpeted boxes that sat at the four corners of the dance floor like the angels of the apocalypse.

John wondered how many hearts were lost or won in the confines of those walls? How many plans were changed by the glimpse of a stranger in the crowd? How many lives were altered by an accidental meeting? It was more than a bar where money was changed into liquor. It was the forge where destiny shaped its metal.

John was leaning against the side counter under an Areca palm that fanned out above him. A track light positioned overhead sent a shaft of light down upon him that made it appear as though he were shrouded in a pillar of smoke. Some men passed by and looked into his eyes wondering why such a handsome man was alone. Others tried to ignore him, making an obvious effort to avoid those eyes and, in so doing, made as much of a statement as those who glared openly.

John, who was never sure of how to react to the attention he received, simply looked straight ahead. As a result some of the men went away thinking that he was arrogant. However, the ones who spoke to him, received the opposite impression. For John was genuinely interested in people. He always looked at them when they spoke; his eyes never strayed to follow a passing boy nor darted about the room. There was no pretense, no flattering remarks to people he didn't like. If he didn't like someone—and that was rare—he avoided talking to him, although he would always politely acknowledge that person.

When Eartha Kitt started to sing, "I don't want to be alone/Where is my man?", another migration began toward the dance floor. John got lost in the music and the words and the fantasy, while keeping an eye on the door to check out all newcomers. Just then there was a commotion and he looked to see what had happened. The new doorman was being verbally crucified for requesting a membership card from a creature in a long black cape that draped down to the floor. The much taller doorman stepped aside and Carlos streamed in, cape flowing behind him. There were appreciative shouts and waves from the dance floor, and he stopped to take a bow. A moment of applause, he moved into the crowd where John was waiting.

"That's what you call an entrance, my dear," Carlos said, pulling off his cloak like Fred Astaire. He twirled it around and laid it atop the counter. "How are you?"

"Just fine. I had a glass of wine and I'm already flying."

"Living dangerously tonight, are we?" Carlos said. Then, looking at his friend from head to boot, he exclaimed, "What HAVE you done to yourself, John. You look so butch. Are you trying to fool the masses or are you simply undecided?"

"I'm flexible, not undecided. There's a difference."

"Yes, if you're a nylon pantyhose. But that's all right, I know how flexible you are. News travels fast in this town. Hello, dear," he said to an older fellow who stopped to kiss his hand. They chatted briefly, and Carlos pulled a card out of his pocket and said, "Do give me a call." The man smiled and walked away.

"I thought you didn't like him," John said.

"I don't. He once asked where Michaelangelo's sixteen chapels were located."

"But you gave him your card."

"It's all right. I gave him the wrong number. Cards with the wrong number in the left pocket. Cards with the right number in the right."

"Sometimes I can't believe you're real." John shook his head in wonderment. "Is Matthew coming?"

"Oh, I'm sure. He probably stopped along the way to give advice to a band of misguided gypsies. Is Bob coming?"

"I don't know what he's doing."

"Did I hit a nerve? A little time away never hurt

anybody. Besides, you have friends. Lovers come and go but friends are forever."

"I know," he said, pulling Carlos into his arms.

"Careful, dear, we don't want them to think we're married."

"I don't care."

"We must keep up appearances at all costs," Carlos said, pulling back.

"Why?" John said adamantly.

"I need a husband," Carlos said through his teeth.

"I thought you were through with love."

"That was last week."

"I think you need to talk to Bob more than I do."

"Darling, I don't need a psychiatrist. Besides, didn't you know, they're all crazy anyway. I told you not to get hooked up with one, he'll drive you bananas. Why didn't you let me fix you up with that nice Colombian flower dealer. He really did like you. Why do you insist on being in love?"

"I don't know, Carlos, that's just the way I am. But tonight is going to be different. Tonight I'm going to dance with a stranger. I'm going to walk up to someone I've never met and ask him to dance."

"That's it; get wild."

"I refuse to stand around and be looked over by people who then only pass by. We're all afraid and nobody's willing to take the chance. How many times have you stood in this very spot and ignored the man next to you because you found him exciting?"

Just then an overweight drunk in a loose, short-sleeved shirt staggered and fell into Carlos' arms. "Excuse me," the drunk said, his breath giving off alcoholic fumes. Then, looking up and seeing Carlos' big round eyes, he said, "Would you like to get fucked?"

"Certainly," Carlos said in his cool, unaffected manner as he pushed the intruder away, "if you can find me a man to do it." Then turning back to John, he said, "Why do people always assume that I'm submissive? Am I wearing the wrong color fingernail polish or something?"

"I don't know," John said politely. "Shall we dance?"

"Of course!"

They danced and talked and looked and listened. Matthew never came but Randy did. He arrived with another young man as small and slender as Carlos. Standing by the telephone, John and Carlos watched them move slowly to the other side of the room, unaware that they were being monitored by anyone. They said "excuse me" as they squeezed by a man in a red shirt who was bouncing to the music in hopes that someone would notice. Randy looked different with a beard, more ominous and foreboding.

"Do you think he can see us?" Carlos asked.

"Can you see him?"

"Yes."

"Well, I guess he can see you, too."

The separation from Randy had left Carlos still feeling unresolved. Not secure enough for another personal contact but not yet released either. He had sent Randy a birthday card with a letter inside that tried to say on paper what he couldn't bring himself to speak. He wrote of how wonderful their being together had been and revealed a number of other equally difficult expressions.

"I'm going to say hello," Carlos said, looking across the room.

"All right. I'm going to ask the guy in the red shirt to dance."

They sauntered in different directions. John went over and stood next to the red shirt who was still bobbing up and down like a float at the end of a fishing line. John waited a few minutes so that it would appear as though he had landed there by chance and then said, "Would you like to dance?"

"Sure," came the response.

"Yes?" John repeated, making sure, then turned and walked out onto the parquet floor. He found a spot and turned to face his partner.

Carlos mingled in the crowd which, by now, was packed in shoulder-to-shoulder so that you had to squeeze through, a practice some enjoyed even more than dancing. Usually John would have gone home by this time, preferring to avoid the oppression of the crowd. Carlos, in contrast, felt right at home. Gregarious by nature, he thrived within the flock, no longer the shy, awkward boy he had been in prep school. Those days were long gone. He had found acceptance and developed his sense of humor so that now others sought acceptance from him. He found Randy paying for the two drinks he had ordered and waited for him to turn away from the bar and hand one to his friend. Carlos felt confident as he approached even if his former friend looked a bit uneasy.

"Hi Randy."

"Carlos. How are you doing?"

"Fine. How are you?"

"Good. Oh, this is Bill," Randy said, seemingly a little embarrassed. "This is Carlos." The two men shook hands, looking each other over without being too obvious.

"I like the beard," Carlos said.

"Thanks. I thought I'd try something new." Randy moved closer to Carlos and spoke low in his ear. "Thank you for the card." Bill looked the other way and took a step toward the wall. Randy continued, "I wanted to respond, but I just didn't know what to say."

"That's all right, Randy. I didn't really expect any reply. To be perfectly honest, that note was more for my benefit than for yours. I needed to get it out, that's all. Is Bill your new boyfriend?"

"Ah, well, I don't know."

"You never could make up your mind, could you?"

Carlos said and watched as Randy's eyes glazed over. Whatever sympathy was in those eyes had suddenly evaporated.
Bill saw Carlos looking at him and stepped closer to Randy.
Randy responded by putting a hand on his new friend's back
and saying, "Carlos is a member of the 500 Club."

"Oh, how interesting. I had thought of joining, but I
have so many other things going on right now."

"Well, maybe I'll see you there some time in the future.
I've got to get back to my friend, so I'll talk to you later."

"Okay, Carlos," the bearded man said. "Take care."

Carlos walked away feeling that he had thrown his pearls
before swine. He was angry but at the same time relieved. He
wondered what he had ever seen in Randy and felt glad that it
was over. Seeing Randy's new friend brought home the
needed sense of completion.

John came off the floor followed closely by the red shirt.
"Thank you," John said. "That was great."

"Yeah, I didn't think I was gonna get to dance tonight,"
his partner said.

"If you were in France, you could dance by yourself."

"There's a guy that comes in here all the time, dances by
himself. He's not here now," the man said, looking around.

"Maybe he's French."

"I've never seen you here."

"It's the only place I come to."

"Well, I don't get out too much," the man admitted.

"What part of New York are you from?"

"Is it that obvious?"

"Takes one to know one. Are you visiting?"

"Hell, no. I got a place down the street. East of the
Boulevard, of course."

"Of course."

"You live around here?"

"Gables," John said.

"That's so far!"

"What? Seventeen minutes by the expressway."

"What'd you do, time it?"

"I did."

"Why do you come all the way here?"

"I like it. My friends are here."

"The only reason I'm here is 'cause it's around the corner."

"The only reason?" John said suspiciously.

"Well, aside from that."

"You're not at Banyan Bay, are you?"

"Hell, no. I bought a house. I don't need a fuckin' condo. It's like livin' in an apartment for cryin' out loud." He put his arm around John. "Would you like to come over? It's right down the street."

"All right," John said and they headed for the door. The tall new doorman smiled at them and said, "Goodnight, gentlemen." John felt obvious.

As they walked out toward the parking lot on the south side of the building, the man asked, "What's your name?"

"John."

He offered his hand, "My name's Larry."

John flinched. "Larry what?"

"Alzeski. Slavic. I'm glad I decided to come tonight."

John slowed down as he reached the car. "Ah . . . ," he hesitated. "I've changed my mind. I think I'm going to go home."

Larry was confused. "I don't understand. What's the problem?"

"No problem."

"Don't I turn you on?"

"It's not that."

"What is it?" Larry was becoming impatient.

"I just can't."

"Well, why the hell didn't you say that inside the bar?"

"Look, I'm sorry."

."You're fuckin' crazy. You better go see a shrink or somethin'."

John stood staring at the ground as Larry walked huffily back toward the bar.

9.

Damn it," John cursed as he reached up from the floor for the telephone. It was Carlos wanting to know what he was up to. They had been out of touch for a few days.

John told him.

"Oh my GOD. That's really kinky. I didn't know you were into that. I thought I was the only sordid one in this group."

"Give it a rest, Carlos."

"Does anyone else know you do this?"

"You're the first."

"I can't believe it. Do you take sugar and cream in your coffee. . . ." Carlos said, laughing hysterically before he could finish the sentence.

"This happens to be a very legitimate cleansing process."

"I used to know a guy who got into wine enemas but he never mentioned anything about cleansings. Used to get drunk as a skunk."

"I'm not drunk. Are you?"

"Say, are you alone?"

"Of course I'm alone," John said belligerently, then he let out a pained groan.

"What's that?"

"Nothing. Just a cramp."

"Are you sure you're supposed to be doing this?"

"Yes, Carlos. I'm getting rid of drug residues stored in my body."

"What drugs?" Carlos was surprised.

"Poppers mainly."

"That's not drugs. I thought you were talking about heroin, mescaline, or acid. That's drugs. You're worrying about nothing."

John thought of his night on acid and decided not to go into it. He let out a frustrated blast of air from his nostrils. "Did you know that nitrate molecules bind themselves to protein molecules and can stay in your body for years?"

"Did you know that worrying about every little thing causes wrinkles that can stay in your body forever. All right, all right, I'll be brief."

"That'll be different."

"The club is bringing someone in Wednesday to talk about 'Living Gay in a Straight Society.' Matthew and I are going. You want to come along? Maybe we'll do something after."

"Sure. Sounds good. What time?"

"Starts at eight, so we can meet there."

"Okay. I'll see you then. I've got to go now."

"I can imagine."

"Bye."

The 500 Club met in the hall of a downtown building just west of Biscayne Boulevard. The room was beginning to fill, as it did once a week, with people who had come to listen to some speaker, however well-known, who could fire them with hope, or rage, or give them encouragement. Matthew, Carlos, and John occupied a table toward the rear. They had been joined by Rick, another regular member who was going to night school to learn how to read. They were sipping coffee. (John's was decaffeinated so that it wouldn't make him nervous.) Rick had arrived earlier to make the coffee and tea and to boil the water for the hot chocolate.

"I see you're using cream this time," Carlos said.

"I always use cream," John looked up from his cup.

"Not always," Carlos reminded him.

John started to flush and figured that the only way to save face was to come right out with it. "I do when it goes in this end."

"What?" Matthew jumped in. "Am I missing something here?"

"Are you ever!" Carlos grinned.

"This is getting interesting," Rick said.

John gave him a dirty look. "Carlos got excited when I told him I put coffee up the rear."

"For medicinal purposes," Carlos lisped and raised his pinky into the air.

"What does it do, give you a high?" Rick asked.

"No. Yes. I'm not doing it for a rush," John said, annoyed.

"I've heard of that," Matthew commented. "Something to do with the caffeine. I'm not sure what it's supposed to do, though."

"Good." Carlos frowned. "Don't get him started. We want to keep this table respectable. Besides, if I know John, he'll go off on some tangent about the acid-alkaline balance and bore us all to tears."

"Stay ignorant. See if I care."

"Give me bliss and a joint any day," Carlos said. "You're the one with six doctors. I told you, the reason you get sick is not because of drugs. It's because you have no preservatives in your system. How do you think I maintain this youthful complexion that men fight over to touch. I'm perfectly preserved."

"You mean embalmed," John said, looking at his demitasse cup.

"Darling, Cuban coffee has kept a nation going for centuries."

"Maybe that's why you're all so volatile."

Carlos gasped out loud and turned to Matthew. "Did you hear that, he called me volatile."

"I heard it."

"I wouldn't harm a fly. I might pull on it a little, but I wouldn't hurt it."

John was still feeling the sting of embarrassment. It was one thing to talk about his private life with Carlos and Matthew but quite another to expose it in public. John was extremely concerned about what people would think. He felt uncomfortable in restaurants when they seated him too close to the next table, and when the waitress brought the check, he always stopped talking. So he was relieved when Rick got up to get more coffee.

"Why did you do that?" John desperately asked Carlos.

"Do what?" Carlos asked back.

"Talk about that stuff in front of Rick."

"You mean your . . . 'habit'?"

"You know what I mean."

"Why are you worried about him?"

"Carlos, people who don't know what's going on might think that's a little abnormal."

"Honey, don't worry about it. People already think you're a little abnormal."

"Given the company he sleeps with," Matthew said.

"I don't consider that abnormal," John stated. "Just different."

"I don't consider it abnormal either," Carlos agreed. "I said 'some people.' Actually, anyone who told me I was abnormal would be giving me a compliment."

"What?" John said, perplexed.

"Sure," Carlos continued. "Abnormal to me means

better than average. Certainly the great minds of our time were not normal."

"That's a good point," Matthew said, impressed at Carlos' depth of vision, which seemed to surface sporadically from beneath his witty, seemingly unconcerned, exterior.

"Why should I feel inferior to anyone or, for that matter, any group?" Carlos shrugged. "I mean, everybody shares the same air, the same sun, the same stream. We come here as equals."

"The only difference is in your head," Matthew added.

"Right," Carlos said, as John nodded thoughtfully.

"And anyone who controls his head, can control his surroundings," Matthew continued.

"Right." For Carlos, the gay experience was nothing more than another learning experience. There was no self-condemnation, no guilt, no difference between homosexual and heterosexual. The difference was in the schoolroom and not in the pupil. If anything, Carlos was proud of his sexual orientation.

"How did we get onto this subject anyway?" John asked, feeling manipulated.

"You were feeling inferior," Carlos said pompously.

"I was NOT feeling inferior. I was feeling exposed."

"What's the difference?"

"There's a big difference." John looked at Matthew for help.

"Are you betraying a confidence, here?" Matthew asked Carlos.

"I didn't say it; he did," Carlos defended himself, as Rick returned to the table with a full cup.

"It's okay," John said, wanting the conversation to end.

"One of these days," Carlos said, feeling sorry for himself, "you're both going to leave me, I know it. Everybody does. That's just the way it is. You'll stay with me for a time; then you'll get mad at me like you are now and you'll go."

"I'm not going anywhere," Matthew said.

"Neither am I," John committed. He was amazed at how intimate their friendship had become in a matter of months and had no problem in promising loyalty.

"But you do make me mad sometimes," Matthew said.

"I do?" Carlos reacted with surprise.

"Yes."

"Matthew!"

"Well, you just said . . ."

"But I didn't think you, too."

"It's not every day, but sometimes you push too hard. I mean you test me. And that's just what it is. You're testing me to the point of anger, and sometimes you go beyond. I think you want to see just how far you can go with me."

"But you're my friend. I simply know I can be myself, that's all."

"No, there are times when you go out of your way to irk me. I've seen you do it to John, too. You just did. It's almost as though you were trying to make sure that we really loved you by doing these awful things, and then if we're still friends afterward, you're satisfied that our friendship is real."

"Oh, baloney." Carlos frowned and looked away.

John drifted off into his own thoughts, wondering if Carlos was right about his worrying too much and being overly self-protective. He had always been so careful. As a young boy, he had been cocky and bold. When his parents took him to visit relatives in the projects on South Street, he rode the elevator down to the lobby and saw an older kid sitting on the windowpane, letting his baseball bat fall repeatedly against the glass. John walked up brazenly to the boy and told him to stop, because it might break the window.

"What do you think I've been doing for the last six months," the boy said defiantly.

"So you're the one," John said, his eyes narrowing.

"I'm the one."

"I'm going to tell the police about this," John said. When he heard that, the boy jumped down and pulled John outside the lobby and into an alley where the rest of his gang was sitting around. John talked confidently to them without suspecting that he was in the slightest bit of danger. They finally let him go and he immediately sought out a police officer who told him to go home to his mother.

What had happened since then to sensitize him? And if he went through that process of becoming more sensitized and cautious, couldn't he also reverse that process and become less so? Suddenly, John was jerked back to reality by Matthew's excited voice.

"Guess who just walked in," Matthew said, and Carlos immediately turned in the direction of the door.

"Don't look." Carlos put a hand on John's arm. "It's Bob. Be discreet."

Bob paid for his entrance and walked in slowly, looking around to see who he knew. He spotted the three friends but stopped to talk with someone before heading in their direction. As usual, he was being overly attentive, his behavior a product of his psychiatric training. When he talked to people, he would reach out to touch them, as he reacted to what they were saying. In this sense, he never stopped working. Finally, he moved on, saying hellos here and there, as he made his way to John's table.

"Hi," he said, smiling at all four of them. "May I join you?"

"Oh," Carlos said, "are we coming apart?"

"Would you join me in a cup of coffee?" Matthew played.

"Do you think we'll fit?"

They're off again, John thought. Rick was hysterical. Bob was only slightly amused. "Sit down." John offered a chair. "We need someone to cheer us up."

"I didn't know you were going to be here tonight," Bob said to John.

"Neither did I. Carlos rounded us up."

Bob turned his head to look at Carlos. "I think you told me about it too."

"I suppose I did mention it."

"You three are getting to know each other pretty well, aren't you?" Bob said, excluding Rick. "I mean you're becoming a real support group. That's great." Then, realizing that he always ended by saying 'that's great,' he added, "I think you're becoming an item of conversation around here."

"So are you two," Rick blurted, meaning Bob and John.

Bob answered, looking directly at Matthew and Carlos. "Why is it that every time two people spend some time together, they're automatically matched up. I don't understand it. We can't enjoy each other's company without people trying to pair us up."

"You're not lovers?" Rick persisted.

"No," John answered, feeling an obligatory need to say this, and at the same time recognizing his pretense. He felt strange, sitting next to the man with whom he was falling in love and denying the fact. All of a sudden there was a vague sense of discomfort in his stomach as he continued with his charade, remembering what he had said to Matthew and Carlos at the Hyatt about love. Now he fervently hoped that they had short memories. "We've only known each other, what?" he looked at Bob, "three months?"

"That sounds right."

"So?" Rick pressed, "my parents only knew each other for five days before they got married."

"Well," Matthew said, "you know how flighty straight people are about relationships."

"One roll in the hay and they're ready for the altar," Carlos said. "How come we can't get married like that? You know, walk down the aisle—the whole bit."

"You can," Rick said.

"Oh, I want it."

"Drink your coffee," Matthew said. "It'll pass."

"I saw Randy the other day at a medical conference," Bob said.

"Better you than me," Carlos responded.

"I take it you're not seeing each other any more?"

"Randy has been relegated to a somewhat nebulous place in my past along with Mickey Mouse and Snow White."

"Onto bigger and better things," Bob said.

"Hopefully true on both counts."

Then Rick looked at Bob and squinted. "How long did you know Nick?"

"Oh, I meant to ask you," Bob said to John as though he had just thought of something extremely important that couldn't wait. "Did you, by any chance, bring the address of that organization you were telling me about in New York that does research on nutrition and psychological disorders?"

"No, I didn't. It's at home. Can I call you at the office with it tomorrow?"

"Okay. Call me in the afternoon, though. I won't be there in the morning."

"What's up?"

"I have to take my car into the shop," Bob said, disgusted.

"What happened?"

"It stopped running. I don't know why."

"Owning a car is like having a relationship," John said. "You have to keep watching it to make sure that all of the things that make it run are still there."

"They convinced me to have the engine overhauled."

"Gotcha," Matthew said.

"Just make sure that they change the air in your tires when you take it in," Carlos instructed. Then he turned to Rick. "So many people run around with the same stale air in their tires year after year. Is it any wonder they have problems?"

"I never knew that," Rick said.

"Oh, my," Carlos frowned. "You must be sure to ask the man at the station to do it for you next time you fill up. It'll only take a minute."

"That's going to cost big bucks," John said to Bob.

"It's cheaper than a new car." He shrugged his shoulders. "Besides, I like it—especially when it runs."

"How long is it going to take?" John probed.

"At least a week. I don't know if I should rent another one or wing it. I have so much to do."

"Why don't you take mine for the week," John offered. "I'm only using it for work, and the bus stops right at my corner." It was a gesture of unity, of coupling, a hope that the two of them would seek each other out in times of difficulty.

"Oh, no," Bob replied, not yet ready for unity and coupling. "I couldn't do that. Thank you. That's a beautiful show of trust, but I'll probably go ahead and rent one."

"Well, if you need it," John said, disappointed, "let me know."

As he spoke the lights went down. John felt relieved to sink into the anonymity of the darkness. Charles Wilson took the microphone, standing on a dusty wooden platform at the back of the room that acted as a staging area. He was a middle-aged man, with a middle-aged spread, who seemed to have no sex life at all. Nor was he ever heard to express a desire for it.

It was his party that John had attended in the Grove with Janet. In a way he was responsible for John's meeting Matthew and Carlos and ultimately, Bob. He was very active in the community and had founded the 500 Club to increase awareness and pride years before such organizations were popular. He remembered the painful process of growing up gay with all its attendant negative programming during those formative years when one begins to crystalize concepts of self image. There was no organization for him to turn to for self esteem and he was beset with a sense of mission to provide an atmosphere of encouragement for others. He had once said of the gay community "They are unaware of their own excellence and tend to believe those who persecute them." His square glass spectacles glittered in the spotlight, and his dark hair was plastered back from his face. He was a likeable sort of fellow, whose exuberance was contagious. The evening's guest speaker was a lobbyist for the Gay Rights National Lobby who had been flown down from Washington D.C. His salary consisted of the plane ticket as well as a room at Charles' house for five days. A great way to get a vacation. The speaker, the lobby, and the club benefited from the arrangement.

After the lecture there was a question and answer period, and the general mood of the thirty-two in the audience grew more relaxed as people talked among themselves and to the speaker. When the questions died down, Charles returned to the platform and thanked the guest. He announced that everyone was welcome to stay for dessert and coffee. Immediately after Charles made that announcement, a young man came out of the kitchen, holding a wide tray with a blue and white cake on it. The cake had a number of candles in it, and their flickering light caused his face to glow in the dark. He strutted proudly between the scattered tables before setting the cake down in front of Bob and John. Everyone began to sing, "Happy Birthday." John was laughing and Bob was shaking his head. John experienced a warm feeling of camaraderie with him.

"I didn't know they were going to do this," Bob said, leaning toward John.

"I had a hunch," John said.

"I'm glad we both came."

Matthew and Carlos smiled knowingly as the honored pair stood in front of the display. The young man presented them with a knife.

"Well, you know," Bob said to the group, "that I can't let this slip by without saying a few words."

"It's the ham in him," John injected and got a laugh.

"I just want to say that this organization and all of the people in it has always been very special to me, and I can't think of a better way to spend my birthday, our birthdays," he shot a glance sideways to John, "than with you."

"That's the truth," John added. "We really didn't expect this."

"Furthermore . . ." Bob continued.

"Just cut the cake," someone yelled.

10.

Janet's apartment was small, but its location made up for everything. Just off Brickell Avenue, it was on the second floor and looked out over Biscayne Bay. Brickell Avenue was the financial district where architects enshrined their triumphs so that generations to come might marvel at their genius; where buildings of black glass and colored concrete were displayed like jewels under glass to bored commuters leaving the downtown area on their way home. It wasn't because Janet made so much money that she was able to live among the wealthy and the famous; it was more a matter of chance. She had found a vacancy in one of the older and smaller apartment houses which, one day, would probably be destroyed to make way for the newer and bigger. The building was privately owned by an old Jewish man who already had as much money as he needed and who liked her immediately.

She had gone to the store earlier for a bottle of French wine, knowing that John wouldn't drink domestic because of the sugar content. She had once accused him of acting worse than a diabetic to which he responded that he'd never have to worry about that. She also juiced three bags of carrots in case he or Bob had a sudden urge for the unusual—a definite possibility among the artistic set.

It had been almost two weeks since John's birthday and this was the first chance she'd had to invite him to the apartment for a celebration drink. Schedules had been tight lately; either she was busy with Anton or John was busy with Bob. Finally, in a flash of insight, she suggested that John stop by with Bob and that way she could meet him and attach a face to the person she had been hearing about so much at the office.

John and Bob walked up the stairs and knocked. "I hope this is the right night," John said when the door opened.

"It sure is." She gave them a glowing smile. "Come in." John walked in ahead of his friend. "This is Bob."

She took his hand. "It's so nice to meet you. I've heard so many good things."

"I have to say the same about you."

John flushed. "All right, it's true. I've been talking about the both of you, so you'll just have to adjust to it."

"No wonder my ears have been buzzing," Janet said. "Can I get you a drink? Some wine?" She looked at John. "It's imported."

"Sounds wonderful," Bob said, feeling the need to calm himself.

"Sit down and make yourselves at home." She went into the kitchen. The two men sat on the couch. On the coffee table was a round tray filled with spokes of celery, carrots, and cauliflower, surrounding a bowl of Janet's famous onion dip.

The room was basic. A sofa and a chair stood against one wall hung with several original paintings, two of which were John's. Two other walls were lined with window-high shelves that held the essentials—stereo, speakers, books, and television. With them and a full refrigerator, one could sustain life for a week.

"Need any help?" John called, when he heard the clinking of glasses.

"No, thanks," she said, emerging with another tray holding three glasses and a bottle. She put it down next to the hors d'oeuvres, pulled up the high back Arthurian chair and sank into its striped, upholstered seat. She raised her glass and said, "To another good year." They touched glasses and then proceeded to lose their inhibitions. The carrot juice stayed in the refrigerator.

"Where's Anton?" John asked. "He should be here to make an even four."

"I told him you were coming, but he had to work late; besides, he wanted to check up on his mother."

"That's the problem. You shouldn't have told him we were coming."

"Oh, stop. You know he thinks the world of you."

"He's a nice guy, Janet. I think you should keep him around."

"You really think so?"

"Yeah. I do."

"Well, in that case, I have something to tell you." She carefully staged the moment which immediately put John on the edge of the sofa.

"Does this have anything to do with your recent streak of treks up to visit the family?" he asked.

"Yes," she grinned and showed them the ring on her left hand.

"Oh, my God," John said. "Engagement?"

She nodded her head with eyes open wide, "He asked me last night."

John hugged her, saying he couldn't believe it, but actually he expected something like this and would have been more surprised if nothing had happened. Bob also warmly congratulated her, and the talk now turned to plans for the wedding. John knew that this would mean changes in their relationship. She would now devote her evenings to Anton. No more Saturday nights dancing under the lights at Uncle Charlie's Disco.

Sitting there, John knew he wouldn't resist the change because he hoped to make a similar connection someday. Though when he thought of it for himself, it seemed more like a fantasy. He wanted it, but he didn't want it. Which of his desires was the stronger, he wondered. With no set goal, he had plodded dreamily along until something happened; then he acted quickly to discourage any intimate involvement. Or at least he had until now. Now he didn't know what course to take as he moved closer and closer toward obtaining his unmentionable dream, and that dream was there, sitting on the sofa in Janet's living room; bone and blood, real.

He turned his attention to Janet. She had been raised in the same sheltered manner as he, and shared many of his values. Suburban Long Island, where she grew up, was a storybook land of houses with picket fences and oak trees that were taller than the residences they shaded.

After graduating from high school, she had left with great fanfare to attend the University of Miami's School of Engineering. After college, she took a job as a draftsperson in the same corporation as John. It was after John had left to study in France that she met Anton who was working as a consultant in the building. He had asked her to lunch one day, and they had struck up an immediate rapport. He'd practically taken up residence at her apartment lately, so things wouldn't be much different after the papers were signed except that they had decided to move eventually into his apartment. It was much larger but lacked the fabulous vistas that Brickell had to offer. John was very happy for his friend. As for Janet, she positively glowed.

When Bob and John left her apartment it was after eleven o'clock. They crossed the street in front of the building and walked along the sea wall. The bay was moving and changing like thousands of bobbing heads in a crowd. Tiny lights glittered and danced across its peaks. As he watched the sparkling water, John was filled with thoughts of life and marriage and love. He began to talk for the first time about his five-year union with Brad.

"Why did you split up?" Bob asked.

"Well, I was young when I met Brad. Twenty-one. I don't think I was really ready for a mature relationship."

"Was he?"

"I think so. He was older than I was. Funny how things work out, isn't it?"

"It sure is."

They had been walking slowly but now stopped to look out over Biscayne Bay. The wind out of the east blew the hair back off of their faces. "Look at it," John said, pointing at the Bay. "There's a feeling of power out there. Did you ever notice how the light plays on the water? I've always thought that life was like so many tropic lights."

"How do you mean?"

"They're always changing. Never static. Neither the moon nor the stars ever stay the same, but they're always there. The funny thing about it is that the moonlight doesn't even belong to the moon. It's only a reflection of something greater. Like a spirit that resides in a body but really belongs under the domain of heaven."

Bob glanced up at the round yellow orb suspended full over the horizon in the satiny sky. A strand of pearl gray clouds hovered directly below.

"Have you ever had a long-term relationship?" John asked.

"Yes. I did."

"What happened?"

Bob let out a sigh, "He joined the Peace Corps."

"The Peace Corps?"

"Yes. We'd been working up to it for a long time. But it's still hard when it happens." Bob looked away. "We decided to end the relationship when he left."

"When was that?" John asked feeling uneasy.

"Six months ago."

"That's all?"

"Yes."

"That's still fairly recent. Do you think you might get together again when he comes out?"

"No." Bob pushed his hair back even though it wasn't in his eyes. "I've pretty well accepted the fact that it's over between Nick and me. We parted on good terms. I still write to him now and then."

"That's good. I see Brad occasionally even though he's living with someone."

"Is that hard for you?" the psychiatrist in Bob asked.

"No. We get along. I've been over for dinner. We don't have a problem that way."

"I don't know if I could do that."

"Of course, Brad and I have been apart for almost six years now."

"I guess that makes it easier." They headed back toward the car. "I was kind of surprised that I reacted to you the way I did," Bob said. "I was steering clear of anything heavy for a while."

"You too?"

"Yes. Sort of an approach-avoidance type of thing, you know? I'm so close to my last relationship that I don't want to get tied down again. But I'm glad that I met you."

"Me too," John answered, not sure of what had really been said. The moon grew smaller as it rose in the night. It wielded its influence on the formless tide below. A group of cumulus clouds drifted in from the east and the moon slid beneath them to light the mist from behind. The fluorescence that filtered through was of a different nature and the tropic lights had changed once more.

11.

Carlos' table was set for three. It looked like a spread out of the glossy pages of *House Beautiful*, everything in its proper place. White cloth napkins were folded beneath gleaming silverware with ornate handles. Glasses, half-filled with red wine, sparkled in the light of two tall white candles in silver holders, one at each end of the table. The glasses themselves were like diamonds that gleamed at certain points. The radiance that passed through the ruby red wine gave it a body and depth that only light could achieve, like a painting by Rembrandt.

An atmosphere of dim refinement pervaded the room as Carlos brought out the chilled beef madrilene for Matthew and John. He warned that the soup was not a typical appetizer, and that some people didn't care for it, but it was a real treat if you acquired the taste. Matthew ate it out of courtesy and actually finished his portion, but John expressed some doubts. While Carlos was checking on the coq au vin and reaching for the black plates with gray bands that he had purchased in Mexico, John seized the opportunity to dump half of his raw beef soup into Matthew's bowl. Carlos returned to the sound of Matthew's astonished laughter. "What's so funny?" he asked innocently.

"I just told Matthew what a slob he was. Look at the way he spilled his soup on his plate."

"Am I going to have to get you a bib?" Carlos asked. "All done?" he said as he took Matthew's half-empty bowl.

"Yes, thank you." Matthew glared at John with a vague sense of having been taking advantage of though he wasn't really sure.

When Carlos took John's bowl he said, "See, that wasn't so bad, was it?"

"It was easier than I thought," John tried hard not to snicker.

Carlos returned with the main course and started chattering away as he set the plates down on the table. He expressed himself as much with his hands as with his tongue—a trait he said he picked up in Italy, but his guests suspected that he probably had the same mannerism forever. When he saw that Matthew's glass was almost empty, Carlos reached for the bottle.

"By the way," Matthew said, "I was talking to Bob the other day."

"Oh, really," John said. "Where was that?"

"Whoa, that's fine," Matthew said, as the glass was about to overflow. "He was at Karleman's. I got there about eleven o'clock, and he was just leaving."

"Who was he with?"

"I don't know. One of the guys from the club, I think. I'd seen him before, but I don't know where."

"It's all right, dear," Carlos patted John on the arm, poured some more wine in his glass, and pushed it in front of him.

"I think they were just friends," Matthew comforted, as John drank his wine. "He's always with friends. I don't think I've ever seen him alone anywhere."

"What do you want from him anyway?" Carlos asked.

"What do you mean?"

"I mean, what's the bottom line, dear? What do you really want?"

"I don't know," John said, pausing to think. "Yes, I do. I want him. I want some kind of a relationship."

"He wants to get married, I knew it!" Carlos threw himself against the back of his chair, saying the words as if he had uncovered a major break through.

"I don't even know if it's that, Carlos. I want something special with him, but it doesn't have to be exclusive. I want people to know that we're together. He could go out with other people if he wanted, but he'd always come back to me. We'd be special to each other, understand each others wants and desires and weaknesses and help each other, you know. I realize that he needs space and that's all right, I do, too. I don't want to crowd him, but damn it, I think I love him."

"I knew you were feeling that," Matthew said. "I was wondering when you would say it."

"Does he know how you feel?" Carlos asked.

"Are you kidding? He goes out of his way to avoid the subject. He won't say a word that even implies attachment. And I am so aware of it. I mean it's obvious that he's holding back. I don't know, I've never felt like this before." John pushed his potatoes to one side of the plate and stared at them. "I really do love him, but I'll tell you something," he said, looking up, "I love him enough to let him go."

"Let him go?" Carlos said, wrinkling his forehead. "What are you talking about? Haven't you ever seen South Pacific? Never-let-him-go. You've got to put everything right up front. I'm telling you. Lay your cards on the line. What do you mean, let him go?"

"He needs freedom. He can't feel tied in. He needs someone there to listen, to comfort him, and to share with him, but it has to be someone who's distant and undemanding." John expelled a long sigh, then said curtly, "I want to be there when he reaches out."

"My God, he thinks he's Joan of Arc. You really should get some grounding, dear."

"What about your needs?" Matthew asked. "It may be that you're ready for a relationship and that you have a lot to give, certainly . . . but he may not be the right one for you, at least not now."

"Yes." Carlos picked up on Matthew's lead. "Maybe he's the symbol of what you're looking for but not necessarily the object."

"He's no symbol," John growled. "I know what I feel. What I don't understand is, I thought that when you're in love it's supposed to make you feel good and nothing else in the world matters. But when I'm with him I'm nervous and unsure. In fact, he makes me feel anxious. Sometimes I don't even know what to say."

"A very wise man once said, 'Sex relieves tension and love creates it,'" Carlos droned in his usual cool, slow, aristocratic tone.

"I just keep thinking about the breakdown I had, and I don't want to go through that again. I don't know how far I can go with this."

"You're doing fine," Matthew said reassuringly. "Just take it from day to day. Don't make expectations that you can't realize. And when anything bothers you, talk to us about it."

"That's right, dear," Carlos said. "You can lean right here on my shoulder. You know," he looked thoughtful, "people who have friends don't need psychiatrists."

"That's very true," Matthew said. "Talking about things is like a . . . like a safety valve on a pressure cooker. I learned that when I volunteered at Switchboard's Crisis Line. They taught us how to listen to people, but anyway, sharing a problem somehow makes it less frightening. I'm not sure how, but it brings things into perspective."

"Reminds me of the old macho image where men can't have problems or express emotion," John said.

"Worst thing in the world," Carlos said, nodding his agreement.

"It's really self-destructive," Matthew continued. "When you don't release all that verbally, it just comes out physically somewhere. You know, of course, that men have shorter life expectancies than women."

"Yes," Carlos said. "I think it's dreadful."

"More men suffer from ulcers and things, too, and it's all related to stress."

"I'm glad I don't have to worry about that," Carlos said.

"That's right," Matthew agreed. "I'm talking about men now."

Carlos raised his chin and looked away.

"That was the most frightening thing I've ever experienced," John said, again referring to his post-drug experience. "People thought I was exaggerating, but I couldn't stop shaking for months. Things that never bothered me before became all-important issues that had to be dealt with. I wasn't sure I COULD deal with them. I really wasn't sure." His eyes began to water and his voice quivered as he spoke. Matthew had stopped eating and was sitting solemnly, holding his fork in his hand. Carlos quietly observed the tension, his face full of concern as he allowed his friend to remember.

"They say that everything happens for a reason, and that when something awful happens, it means there's an area of your life not yet in order, and the experience shows you what it is you have to change to go on. And okay, in the long run the result was positive: It forced me to give up drugs and sugar and all that stuff and to start taking better care of myself. Overall, looking at it without any emotion, it was good for me. But going through it was like passing through hell. At the time there was no way that I could see any good coming of this thing. It was a difficult time in my life. It was THE most difficult time in my life. I have never had to reach down so far into myself and fight to survive as I did then. I don't think I could describe to you what the feeling was like. It's incommunicable. Have you ever had an experience that was so profound, so utterly devastating that it either destroys you or changes you forever?" Though he asked the question, he did not expect them to be able to respond. No one else could have gone through such a purging by fire.

"Yes," came the answer. "I have," Matthew said quietly. "When I tried to commit suicide."

John was struck speechless. That single sentence delivered with such calm control hit him with a force that was almost physical so that his head actually jerked back in response. In an instant he became aware that someone else had suffered the unsufferable and survived. That he was not alone in his trial was a revelation that sent his head spinning. A wave of emotion welled up within him and he experienced a sense of deep kinship with Matthew that he had not previously allowed himself. Meanwhile, Matthew sat quietly at the head of the table, quite unaware of the impact of his words. When the three of them had first formed their alliance, it was always John and Carlos who talked about their problems to Matthew. He was the great mediator. He always listened and counseled, but never spoke of his own needs and feelings outside of whom he thought to be the most beautiful man at Joseph Patterson's party in Surfside. And now here he was revealing this private innermost layer of himself.

"When I found out that Larry was going out on me, I was a mess. Walking around like a zombie. I couldn't express any emotion. I hadn't laughed in years, didn't cry, didn't feel sorry for anyone. Except maybe myself. I was blocking my emotions. You see, I was the one who had made the effort to start that relationship and to keep it going. I made all the moves." Matthew picked up the salt shaker and turned it in his hand.

"How'd you find out he was unfaithful?" John asked.

"Well, I knew for some time. Then one day I came home

from work. We had different hours. I wasn't feeling well. My ulcer was acting up, and I found him in my bed with someone else."

"How dramatic," Carlos said.

"What did you do?"

"What COULD I do? I was angry. I was pissed. That guy got out of there real fast."

"I'll bet," Carlos said.

"I was hurt, and I was disgusted, and I was afraid—all at the same time. I was in a state of crisis; most of all I wanted to teach them both a lesson. I stayed that way for a week. One day something happened, and I got mad and threw a fit. I broke the furniture, started sceaming. Larry'd never seen me act like that before. To tell the truth, I never had. Then I felt guilty for losing my temper. You know, I wasn't being the perfect human being that I thought I was supposed to be."

"Yeah, those ideals we have to live up to," John said.

"Right and I wasn't doing that. So it only made me more upset. Remember, I was still mad at him and still wanted to make him sorry for what he did to me. So one night I took the tranquilizers out of the cabinet; there were about twenty of them left. I didn't know if twenty would do it, but I took them all anyway. I was going to make him see what it would be like without me around any more." Matthew sat gazing into the salt shaker as if it held him entranced.

"What a strange feeling that must have been," John said. "Not knowing whether you would ever wake up or what reaction it would cause."

"Well, I looked for something else to take with it, just in case. I had some muscle relaxers, too, so I swallowed them, figuring it would help me to relax."

"Were you afraid when you took them?" John asked.

"I wasn't afraid, I was angry. As they began to take effect something came into my head. I thought, damn, why was I letting HIM do this to me? And in that moment I realized that

Larry was the cause of all this failure, not me. He was doing it. Everything that was going wrong with the relationship was going wrong because of him—not me. I was blaming everything that happened on myself, his going out with other people, the distance between us, the arguments. Everything. And all along it was him. I had this revelation as I was drifting off to die. And in that second I decided that I didn't want to do this to myself. I wanted to live. By this time I could barely talk, but somehow I managed to find enough strength to call out to Larry."

"He was there?" Carlos gasped.

"Oh, yes, he was in the living room, but he knew that I was mad, and he was keeping his distance. Oh, he was there all right. I called out to him and told him to go to the store and buy some Syrup of Ipecac."

"What's that?"

"It makes you vomit. The last thing that I remember was bending over the sink throwing up."

"And at no time during this whole thing did you become afraid?" John said. He felt instinctively that, knowing everything about Matthew's story would help him through his own dilemma.

"Yes, I did, when I decided I wanted to live because I thought it might be too late. But my panic helped me to fight off the effect of the sedatives. Then I remember being ice cold and wondering if I was dead. I was in the hospital emergency room. Sensations began to return to me slowly, and I became aware of noises in the distance. Later, I was aware of lights, and I called out. A nurse came over and told me where I was, and I said I wanted to go home. She said no, and I started to get up. She pushed me down easily with the tip of her fingers. It didn't take much to control me, I was so weak. Finally, they decided to let me go. The only reason the police weren't called in, and I wasn't put in Jackson for three days of observation, was because I had stopped the attempt myself.

"When I made that decision lying there in bed fading away it was, in a way, the high point in my life. Or it was a turning point, I should say. It was like a part of me opened up, and I knew what life was about."

Matthew paused. Like a good actor, he knew he had his audience's complete attention. He put the shaker firmly down on the table as if to emphasize his point.

"In the twinkling of an eye, my whole existence had been changed, I had found myself in hell. Yet it was precisely at this moment that I vowed to lift myself up from hell and into the heaven where I belonged. It was on that hospital bed that I developed a belief that there is power in one's own will. It is by our very own hand that we arrive at today, via the thoughts that we entertained yesterday. And it's like I keep telling you, John, if you don't like where you are, then you have to make the choice to leave. No one else can take you by the hand and, like Virgil, lead you out of Hades." He shook his head slowly. "The average Joe on the street is worried about his apartment and his salary and his boyfriend who cheats on him but I think that the greatest men live more within themselves. We can transform ourselves only because we can change our thinking."

"You realize that you are going against established thought when you say that," Carlos said. "I mean everybody figures that you're happy because you have money or a lover, not the other way around."

"I know that. Why do you think there are so many unhappy people?"

"When did all of this happen to you?" John asked.

"Well, let's see, about three years ago."

"That's the same time I went through my crisis."

"Late summer, August, I guess it happened then."

"My God! That's a month before. We were experiencing this at virtually the same time without knowing each other. I was hoping it was much earlier for you. You seem to be so much in control of it. I still think about it."

"You're different from me though," Mathew said, thoughtfully. "You hold on longer. I let things go. That's all part of what I meant about changing thought patterns."

"Yeah, I guess that's true. I do hold on for a long time."

"I suffer when I'm going through it, but then when it's over, it's over. I go on to other things. You keep it inside of you. You relive it again and again. That's no good."

"Yeah," John thought about it.

Then Matthew added, "Injuriarum remedium est oblivio."

Carlos leaned toward John and whispered teasingly, "I didn't know he was bilingual."

"What does that mean?" John asked.

"It means, 'Forgetting trouble is the way to cure it'."

"Sometimes it's hard to forget," John said.

"Sometimes it is," Matthew agreed.

There was a long pause, then Carlos became animated again. "Well, anyone for dessert?"

"What is it?"

"It's not your typical dessert," he warned. "But once you've developed a taste for it . . ."

Hearing those familiar words, John fell back against his chair and looked at Matthew.

12.

Bob packed his shaving gear and toothbrush in a travel bag and headed for John's apartment. They went to a movie in Kendall and held hands in the back row. Afterward, still warmed by the intimacy and feeling good from the picture, they came back to the apartment to make love and fall asleep in each other's arms. Music from a thousand strings washed softly over them as they lay together. Layers and folds of soft sheets bunched around and over like the beautiful petals of a flowering Hibiscus. The night was still, disturbed only by the rustle of leaves in the breeze that gently ruffled the orchid trees. Shadows created by the street light splashed against the windows.

Sleeping with Bob was the imagined vision coming to life, the thing he dared not hope for, which had lived only in fantasy. John was always comparing himself to other people who seemed to be happier, healthier, and generally better off. Other people seemed to find relationships with ease flowing out of one and into another in relatively little time. Since he left Brad, John had been on his own, finding occasional affairs, but not achieving the permanence that he idealized.

As a result he had begun to doubt his own capacity to love and was afraid of becoming jaded in a world of temporary affairs and physical lust, where value was placed first on the size of his machinery and only second on the treasures of his soul. But John's doubts were melting away as he lay beside his silent lover. The touch of Bob's skin as they lay curled in embrace stirred in him an emotion that seemed to come from another world, another mind. He knew deep inside that his love was lasting; not just something that might be possible, it was real. This new feeling was a revelation—that he could love again. But such a revelation, while sometimes reassuring, was at others so profound that it frightened him. He was opening doors that led to his deepest subconscious, doors that had been shut and secured for a long time. Now he would have to come face-to-face with the darkness imprisoned there, but he was willing to do that—to open himself up to the light. There had been times when Bob was fast asleep and he had lain awake to enjoy their closeness only to find himself suddenly struck with terror. At such moments he wondered how he could handle this situation and what would become of it and him? Then adrenalin would rush into his veins and he would hyperventilate as he lay secure, yet terrified, with Bob's sleep-warm arms wrapped around him.

Morning came softly, and the sound of crickets gave way to the singing of mockingbirds and the chattering of wild parrots in the trees. Sunlight spilled into the little room, and where it passed through the wide banana leaves outside the door, it shone green. The neighbor's cat was howling for its breakfast and the smell of bacon and coffee was filtering in from the landlady's window. John stared up at the ceiling, hands behind his head, thinking about sharing holidays with Bob and taking him to his brother's house for Sunday dinners. He was sure they'd get along. When Bob stirred, he kissed him and said good-morning. They lay peacefully entwined, as Bob crossed that middle-ground between sleep and waking. It was the weekend, and neither of them had to work. When they did get up, it was at their own pace. John let his lover have the bathroom first. When John came out, rubbing his face with the towel, Bob was in the living room.

"This is an interesting painting," Bob said, looking at one of the pieces on the east wall.

"I did that when I was in France."

"You lived there for a while, didn't you?"

"A year, and this was the last painting I did there."

"I like the blending of the colors. You're very good at knowing which ones to use. Are the figures anyone you knew, or did they come out of your imagination?"

"It's more of a concept really. They're two lovers standing there, and you can't see the line that separates them because they are one. They're merged together through their love for one another."

"Very ethereal."

"I like it very much, too. My paintings are almost a part of me and I hate to sell them sometimes."

"I can understand that, although I'm not an artist."

"You getting hungry?" John asked, moving toward his windbreaker.

"Yes, you ready to go?"

"Yeah." John made a quick detour to the kitchen, swallowed a handful of vitamins, then followed Bob out the door. They walked toward Ponce de Leon Boulevard, only a block away. Orchid petals were falling in a gentle rain of violet that carpeted the sidewalk giving John reason to park his car on a side street. The sky beyond the orchid trees was a brilliant blue with a quality of light unique to this part of the world. They went into a coffee shop at the Chateau Bleu Hotel and sat at a window that looked out onto the street. They could see across to the little triangular park, that had a fountain dedicated to Juan Ponce de Leon, surrounded by stone benches and roses planted by the Garden Club of Coral Gables. Throughout breakfast Bob was tense and, finally, pushing aside his coffee cup, he said that he needed to talk about something that was bothering him. John leaned forward in his seat.

"I thought that I was handling things pretty well but I guess I'm not," Bob's words came slowly and he looked down as he spoke. "I'm still a little too close to my breakup with Nick. I guess what I'm saying is that I'm feeling a need for more space. When you were talking about the painting, it really hit me."

"But I wasn't referring to us. I painted that years ago in Aix."

"I know but it still says something about you that is very beautiful, but which I really can't deal with right now. And when I talked with you on the phone last week and I said that I was going out with Randy, you thought that something was going on between us. I was starting to feel guilty about it, as though I had to explain myself, even though nothing was happening. I don't want to feel tied down right now, and I'm starting to feel that way. I have a need for some space. At least, for a while."

The sunlight that filtered through the tinted window changed its intensity as huge white cloud masses passed overhead, throwing shadows that flickered across the restaurant.

"So do I," John responded. "I'm not trying to close in on you. It's true, I think you're very special, but I'm not looking for a monogamous relationship right now either."

"You aren't?"

"No."

"That's good to hear, although I'm not saying that something like that won't ever be possible."

"I understand that," John said.

"Just not now. I mean, I believe in monogamous relationships only because that's the way I am. Someday I will probably settle into one again. I'm sure that I will. It's simply too soon." He sighed in some desperation. "Am I making any sense?"

Without thinking, John said the only thing he could. "Yes, you're making a lot of sense."

"I think we should see other people too, you know, to broaden our horizons."

"I don't have any problem with that," John conceded.

"It'll be good for me to get away next week. Help to sort things out."

"Where are you going?" John was surprised by the news, but accepted it as part of the whole turn of events.

"A friend of mine invited me and another associate that we both know—a lady—" he specified deliberately, "to come down to his cottage in Key West."

"That sounds great," John tried to be excited. "How long are you going to be away?"

"Only a week. I would have invited you too, but we had made the plans months ago, and I think June wants to talk, so. . . ."

"You don't have to apologize. It'll give me a chance to catch up on some canvases that I left unfinished."

"Oh, good. I'll give you a call as soon as I get back. Maybe I'll get to see the finished product."

"You finished?" John said, collecting the check.

"Oh, let me help."

"No, no. You got the last one."

They both walked out into the dappled sunlight.

13.

The moon over Miami cast an eerie glow on the tops of the palm trees. Its effect on people was almost as well documented as its effect on the tides. A police officer once told John that the department was at its busiest during a full moon. Matthew had confirmed it, recalling that the crisis lines at Switchboard were unusually busy on a night such as this one. A soft breeze blew across the Coconut Grove Yacht Basin and into the downtown section of the village where old-fashioned street lamps lighted the tiled sidewalks. Weekends in the Grove were always special and Matthew, Carlos, and John decided to catch the comedy at the playhouse in order to keep John's mind occupied with anything but Bob's escape to the Keys. After the final curtain they left the theatre and headed down Main Highway toward Hattie's for a drink. Carlos had already had a few before the play and another two during intermission. He was well on the way to his own form of painless oblivion. As they walked, he made astute but rather loud observations about the people they passed. "See this guy," he pointed to an older gentleman with a woman on his arm who looked like she had just come out of church, "I saw him at the baths the other day. Hello there, remember me?" Then to Matthew, "I guess he doesn't remember."

They entered Hattie's long pink room and sat down at the bar. John was on the left, next to a tall figure standing against the counter with a bottle, Carlos was in the middle, jabbering away, and Matthew was on the right, beside a young punker whose back was toward him. They overhead the young man with a safety pin in his ear, tell a friend about how he was mugged the other day. Carlos leaned over to Matthew and said, "Poor thing, they hustled him down to the ground, took his wallet, and died his hair."

"What are you drinking?" John asked, getting ready to order.

Carlos said, "I'll have a white wine."

"Are you sure you want more wine?" John asked. "You wanna try a soda and lime?"

"No. I want wine," Carlos said politely but loudly.

"How 'bout you Matthew?"

"I would like a Moosehead."

"A what?" Carlos drew back.

"A Moosehead," Matthew said, "I would like a Moosehead."

"Are they going to know what I'm talking about if I just say Moosehead or am I going to be embarrassed?" John asked uneasily.

"Of course. It's a beer. They'll know."

"I have never heard of anybody walking into a gay bar and ordering a Moosehead."

"Trust me," Matthew grinned.

"Said the spider to the fly," Carlos kicked in.

"All right," John turned, placing his trust in Matthew's experience. The bartender stood before him, poised, pleasant-faced, her eyebrows raised in anticipation.

"One soda and lime," he pointed to a spot in front of himself. "One white wine and one . . . Moosehead."

"What was that last one?" she leaned toward him.

John glanced uncomfortably at Matthew and then back at the waiting girl. "A Moosehead?" he questioned, feeling ridiculous.

"A MOOSEHEAD," she repeated with emphasis.

"What are you talking about? This is a bar, not a curio shop."
John's face was red; then she broke out in a stream of laughter
and grabbed his arm. "I'm only kidding. I heard you talking,"
she said. "Coming right up."

Matthew and Carlos thought that was uproariously
funny, and Carlos couldn't stop laughing, no doubt the wine
had something to do with his attack of humor. Pretty soon the
three of them were being monitored by the tall man standing
next to John with the beer in his hand.

"Do you always create this kind of a disturbance when
you go out?" he said to John.

"Only when I'm with them," he nodded to his right.

"They bring out the worst in you, I take it."

"Or the best, I'm not sure."

"Name's Douglas," the man put out his free hand.

"John," he said and looked at his two friends, but they
were lost in their own conversation, so he turned back to
Douglas.

"You usually don't come in here, do you?" Douglas
asked.

"We saw the play and decided to stop in for a drink."

"How was it?"

"It was entertaining. I wouldn't go see the movie
though."

"I don't get to see too many plays. My company keeps me
busy." Douglas took a sip of his beer.

"What do you do?"

"Make cardboard boxes. You may not suppose there's
much of a demand for that but I think you'd be surprised. We
make everything from gift boxes to crating packages. Father
died and left me the whole damned business. Takes up every
hour I got. But it lets me drive around in a Porsche and live on
Brickell."

"Sounds like business is booming," John was glib.

"You got that right. All the world wants cardboard. Can you imagine how different your life might be without it?"

"I guess it would be." John thought of a day without cardboard. The man in the plaid shirt was tall and interesting—an earthman—not the kind of person he had expected to meet in the pink room. John wanted to learn more about cardboard, but in the background he could hear Carlos saying in a voice that was clearly audible, if a little slurred, "How much you want to bet John gets laid tonight?"

John continued to talk and didn't turn around, hoping that if he ignored him, Carlos would move on to something else.

"I know he's gonna snag this guy."

John found it hard to concentrate on what the man was saying and wondered if Douglas too had heard Carlos.

"They'll be out of here in twenty minutes or less, watch."

John reeled around, forgetting the plaid shirt. "Will you be quiet!" he commanded.

"Uh-oh," Matthew said. "I think he's getting angry."

"Is that right, John?" Carlos said. His dark eyes met John's. "Are you angry?"

"Yes, I am," John replied steamily.

"Okay. You wanna be angry? You can be angry. But what's the pay off? What are you gonna get out of it, huh?"

They looked at each other in silence for a tense minute that seemed longer than it was. "You're drunk," John said and started to walk angrily toward the door.

Carlos called after him, "I make twice your salary. I can afford to be drunk."

The door closed behind him.

"He's really upset," Matthew said. There was a long silence in which neither of them spoke. Douglas, who had watched impassively, turned back to the counter. "I hope he'll be all right," Matthew continued.

"So what am I supposed to do, feel guilty?" Carlos aid belligerently. "I got a little carried away, big deal. He's gotta grow up some day if he wants to make it in business. I refuse to feel guilty anymore, Matthew."

"I'm not asking you to feel guilty."

"I'm giving it up."

"I'm just concerned, that's all," Matthew said, looking down at his drink.

"I tried to get him to talk about his anger, and he told me I was drunk."

"I know."

"What kind of a friend is that? I know I'm drunk but I'm not gonna go home and let him spoil my evening."

"Well, I've had enough. Are you going to be able to drive?"

"I'm fine, dear. I'm going to stroll over to the Pub."

"All right then. I'll talk to you later," Matthew said and left.

It was three o'clock in the morning, and John was doing situps on the living room floor. Every light in his apartment was on to dispell the darkness. He had already run around the block twice. The hands on the clock passed so slowly as though time itself had been altered. He heard a sound of footsteps on the sidewalk, and he shrank into a corner. His eyes jumped about the room, while his head remained stationary. He bolted the door shut, closed the windows, pulled down the shades, and put on some soft music. After a minute he went to the refrigerator, got out a bottle of wine, and then immediately put it back again. He thought of the Valium in the medicine cabinet, but then remembered about mixing drugs. Thoughts kept jumping randomly in and out of his head.

He remembered what had happened earlier that evening at Hattie's and the event seemed to take on paramount proportions. The confrontation played over and over in his mind; each time the consequences became increasingly threatening. He heard a truck pass on a distant street, and jumped. The situation with Carlos was unresolved and would remain that way for several days because Carlos was scheduled to go out of town on business. To be upset and unresolved at a time like this was definitely a matter of crisis. He paced the living room floor, thinking of Matthew asleep in bed. He walked over to the phone and looked at it, stroking it along the receiver, then walked away. If he called, that would be admitting something was wrong. He could handle it. He could handle it.

He decided that just talking to his friend would be all right. But no, it would get Matthew out of bed. No one calls a friend at three o'clock in the morning unless they're in trouble. He wasn't in trouble. He could handle it. He slowly picked up the phone, trying to think of something else. The drawer opened, and he pulled the address book out. Turning to G, he found the number. He pressed each button slowly and deliberately, stopping before he pressed the last number. He waited a while then pressed it. The phone rang once, twice. He felt so guilty. Three, and he put his finger over the receiver button. On the fourth ring a groggy voice came on. "Hello."

"Matthew?"

"Yes. Who is this?"

John wanted to hang up but it was too late. "John," he said and committed himself to the call.

"What's the matter, John?"

"I'm sorry I woke you."

"It's all right. I don't have to go in until late," Matthew lied. "What's the matter. Are you all right?"

"I don't know what happened tonight. I got mad. Maybe I shouldn't have left."

"You did what you had to do. I understand that. I didn't feel very good about it."

"What did Carlos say?"

"He was upset but . . ."

"Oh, Jesus!"

"John, is something wrong?"

"I, umm."

"What?"

"I'm scared." Silence.

"Of what?"

"After I left you I went someplace else and I met someone. He came over and we smoked some grass. It was sensemillia. I didn't know. I think I'm having a reaction. God knows what else was in there. What should I do?"

"Don't worry. It'll be all right. It will pass eventually. Just relax. Don't get yourself worked up over it; that'll only make things worse." Matthew tried to speak calmly.

There was a groan from the other end.

"If you relax and just flow with it you'll be fine. Try to enjoy the feeling."

"I feel weird, Matthew."

"That's all right. It's nothing to worry about. It's just your body reacting to the chemical. You'll pass it out soon."

"How soon? How do I get it out?"

"Relax. Calm down, John." He sounded like a kind doctor, soothing an hysterical patient.

"Matthew, I never reacted to pot like this before."

"Well, this is a little stronger, that's all. Think about something else. Don't think about the drug. What did you do today?"

"I, ah, worked on a new design for a book cover."

"And were you happy with it?"

"Yes. But my boss doesn't like art deco. He doesn't, um, should I drink some milk? Will that calm me down?"

"You can drink some milk if you want." Matthew sounded definite and knowing.

"Wait a minute," John put the phone down and rummaged through the refrigerator. He found the carton behind the bean sprouts and tofu and poured it into a small glass. He raised it to his lips with both hands and drank the whole thing in one gulp. Then he ran back into the living room and picked up the phone. "There, maybe if I get my metabolism going it'll work it out faster."

"John, you're going to be all right, believe me."

"God, it's so dark outside."

"John, did you hear what I just told you?"

"What, that I'm going to be all right?"

"Yes. You are. Do you believe what I'm telling you?"

"I think so." John sounded more than a little vague.

"Say it, John. I'm going to be all right."

"I'm going to be all right." He repeated the words weakly.

"Again. And think about what you're saying." Matthew's voice sharpened.

"I'm going to be all right," John said a little louder and slower.

"Good. Now just keep that thought in mind, and when you think of anything else, go back to that thought until you believe it."

"All right Matthew. I'll be O.K. now." He didn't want to keep his friend up any longer. Even in crises he didn't want to inconvenience anyone else. He was only learning to reach out for help, and doing it was still embarrassing and awkward. It was his problem, and there was no sense in bothering Matthew any longer.

"I know you will."

"I'm sorry I woke you up."

"I'm glad I was here for you."

"Good night." John hung up and stretched out on the couch. The lights were still on and the stereo was playing something unobtrusive. Like a magical chant, he kept repeating Matthew's words, knowing that his friend was there if he needed him again. That made him feel safer, and he wondered

how long it would be before he became afraid again. Then he
fell asleep, exhausted.

It was well into the week and usually by Wednesday
Matthew was caught up enough to leave the office on time. He
came back to the empty house, threw a couple of hamburgers
on the skillet and made a salad for himself. No more than five
minutes after he finished eating, the phone rang. Ever since he
put two pieces of masking tape on the bells, it rang quietly. He
smiled at the sound as though he had triumphed against the
phone company for a change. Putting his dish in the sink, he
walked to the living room and picked up the receiver. "Hello."

"Hello," came a muffled voice that sounded far away as
though the speaker were not talking into the mouthpiece.
"This is the operator. I have a long-distance call coming
through, will you accept the transmission?"

"Yes, I will." Matthew had instantly recognized Carlos'
disguised voice.

"Thank you. By the way young man, I cut in on your last
call, and I'd watch it if I were you. The telephone is not a toy.
Go ahead Miami." There was the second of two electronic
beeps and an excited voice came on. "Hello Matthew. It's
Carlos."

"Hello, Carlos," Matthew said dryly. "By the way,
Miami is not a long-distance call."

"Well, for the amount of time I have spent to get to your
house, it ought to be. What are you doing?"

"Not too much. Washing dishes. Larry's at the office with
a client . . ."

"At this hour?"

"Well, they couldn't come in at any other time, so I'm
enjoying my solitude."

"That's good," Carlos said. "I called you last night but
your line was busy."

"Last night. Oh, I called John to see how he was doing."

"Oh, and how is he doing?" Carlos was elaborately casual.

"Fine. He just bought a new suit for Janet's wedding, and he was wearing it while he described it to me."

"Dressed to call."

"Exactly."

"Did he mention anything about the other night?" Carlos had imagined some dramatic change of behavior in John since 'the other night', and was fishing for some clue.

"We talked about it a little bit."

"He's stewing, right?"

"No. I don't think it's that big a deal, and I told him so."

"You told him. So evidently he does think it's a big deal."

"No, I didn't mean that."

"So, what did he say?"

"He didn't say that much, actually. If you want to talk to him, why don't you call him?" Matthew wasn't going to make it easy for Carlos.

"No. I'm not going to call him until he stops sulking. Until that happens there's no sense in talking to him. When he's feeling better, he'll call me."

"I don't think he's sulking, Carlos."

"Well, I'm glad to hear that. I'm glad that nothing's changed between us. And if nothing's changed, he's got to call me sooner or later."

"And then the two of you can continue to talk and chatter as usual and pretend that nothing happened."

Since the scene at Hattie's Carlos and John had not spoken to one another. A gulf of uncertainty had formed between them as each was unsure of the reactions of the other. John was clearly aware of the rift in their friendship, and knew that he, for one, would continue to feel uncomfortable until it was resolved. After all, Matthew had told him that he held on to his hurts too long. Carlos was also aware of the tension but felt that, since he was the one who had been attacked, the first move should be made by John.

Meanwhile they both waited, each wanting a truce, each willing to be approached, but remaining separate. John's discomfort with an unresolved issue, however, was greater than his sense of wounded pride, and so finally, he went to see Carlos.

He parked outside the townhouse in the space marked Visitor, locked the door, and walked around to the entrance that read 213. He climbed slowly up the tunnel of a staircase and rapped at the door at the top.

"Just a minute," came a voice from inside. The latch turned and the door opened. Carlos flinched and smiled. "John," he gave a nervous chuckle. "Come on in, dear. I thought you'd gone to live in Timbuktu."

"No, no. I'm still here, like the heat and the roaches."

"I'm glad to see you. Sit down. Can I get you a tonic?" Carlos asked, ever the host.

"No thanks, but go ahead and have something for yourself."

"Well, maybe a little something just to be sociable." He went to pour himself a drink and came back and plopped down across from John.

"I thought maybe we could clear a few things up that are on my mind."

"Okay." Carlos braced himself for the worst.

"I was really upset with you the other night at Hattie's, and I think it's important that we talk about it so that I don't turn it into resentment or anything."

"Go ahead."

"I just don't think it was very good of you to embarrass me like that in front of someone that I was trying to impress. You were talking very loudly, Carlos, and we could both hear you. And only a few days before it happened, Matthew and I had been talking about how important it was to express your anger instead of keeping it inside of you, and that's why I turned and said that I was angry. Maybe any other time I would have ignored you. I think that it was really the liquor that was making you talk like that."

"It was . . . and I'm sorry if I got out of hand. I get that way sometimes when I've had too much to drink."

"It wouldn't have been so bad if you had said it to Matthew or to me but everybody heard it. Everybody in the damned bar."

"I didn't realize then that I was being loud, but I knew you were upset," Carlos said quietly. "You had a right to be, but why did you walk out? That's what I don't understand. I mean, we're supposed to be friends, John. You stormed out of there like I was some idiot on the street not worth dealing with."

"I was mad and I was embarrassed."

"Yes, but you could have just told me. I would have listened. You always run away from situations."

"No, I don't," John defended.

"You do so. You ran away from Brad. You ran away from that other guy that you got involved with a couple of years ago, the drug guy."

"What was I supposed to do, stay there and be humiliated?"

"You weren't being humiliated. We could have worked it out right there. I was trying to do that when you walked away from me."

"I didn't see it that way. I thought you were being confrontational by asking me what the pay-off was for being angry."

"I wasn't. I was trying to analyze your feelings."

"Oh, come on, Carlos. You were drunk."

"I wasn't incoherent."

"Well, I guess neither of us came across very well that night." John studied his hand.

"I guess not." There was a pause, and Carlos wondered if he had said the wrong thing by agreeing. "Look. I'm really sorry the whole thing happened." He gazed at the floor. "I value your friendship and I hope this doesn't damage what we have."

That was all it took to soften John and make him see Carlos in the same old light. The old feelings of warmth returned, at least on a surface level. "Yeah, me too," he said finally. "But I don't always run away. I mean I came here, didn't I?"

Carlos smiled, realizing that John had been influenced by his words. "You sure did. You must be getting better. Probably has something to do with the company you've been keeping."

"Maybe." They looked at each other for a moment and didn't know what to say. They both felt awkward now that all had been cleared and it seemed somehow inappropriate to speak of mundane things, so John reached out and patted Carlos on the side of the shoulder and said goodnight. He walked slowly toward the door, feeling there was something else he should say, but he could think of nothing. Carlos watched him descend the stairs into the parking lot. He didn't close the door until John was out of sight. Then he walked over to the wall unit, put Donna Summer on the tape deck, and cleaned the bathroom.

14.

John continued to see Bob and Bob continued to be elusive but available. They got together on an average of twice a week, sometimes more, sometimes less. Sometimes they didn't see each other at all and John wondered if all relationships operated in the same sporadic way. He had seen couples at parties who appeared to be inseparable and for the first time he entertained the idea that perhaps they only seemed to be inseparable. There must be spaces in every romance, just as there are spaces between each day but how much was typical?

One evening during a heavy fall rain, Bob said that he was again planning a trip to the Keys to get away from the city and the routine. He needed some time by himself to recharge and a week at his friend's cottage in Key West seemed to be the perfect solution. John had often told him that he was working too hard, seeing too many patients, and said it would do him good to relax for a change. He encouraged Bob to go while he covered his own wound. Bob said he would call as soon as he returned and they would get together.

So once again they were separated by the Straits of Florida and John found ways to keep himself occupied. Hands clasped behind his head. Down to the right, elbow touches knee and up. Down to the left, elbow touches knee and up. One, two, three, one. The radio pounded in the background. One, two, three, two. Ten, fifteen, twenty. Breathing heavily.

A twenty-watt bulb shone over the stereo and illuminated John, but left the rest of the apartment in shadow.

He stood in front of the mirror, watching himself, concentrating on his physique as mind and body worked together to bring about the desired result. He wore nothing but his sneakers, because of the tiny lift he kept in the right side. A chiropractor had shown him an x-ray of his spine that was curved because his right leg was imperceptibly shorter than his left. "It's very common," the chiropractor had said. "But if you wear this little jobbie, it'll set your frame level again."

John stood motionless, studying the curves reflected in the mirror and passing his hand over his chest, feeling the rises and depressions of his body. His hand moved down over his abdomen and across his thigh. He remembered the way Bob had touched his hips and the tingling sensation it had created. He remembered the way Bob kissed the hairs on his stomach that divided his torso and pointed down between his legs. He touched himself and remembered Bob. The image in the mirror faded as his thoughts focused and zoomed in on the man with the blonde hair. The vision was all consuming as John fell onto the couch, legs stretched forward and head back in ecstacy. His body tingled in every atom; every particle of his being was charged. The night was softly alive: a banana leaf rapped against the awning in the breeze, a cricket chirped in the brush, looking for another cricket, and the radio mellowed to "Unchained Melody" as he fell asleep in the peace of exhaustion.

Matthew had thought about moving for a long time. But there was something unsettling about doing something you've never done before. He had lived with his older brother, and between them, they had raised their younger sister. From there he went to live with his aunt and immediately after that, he had moved in with Larry. The prospect of his own apartment filled him with uncertainty. There were times when he thought of all of the things he could do in an apartment that he couldn't do at the house, like having guests over, or spending a quiet evening cuddling in front of the fireplace with a date, or any of the other things that Carlos and John could do. They told him of the wonders of privacy, and he was willing, even eager to explore.

But, of course, Carlos wanted to be married and John wanted to move in with Bob. How wonderful could living alone be if they were so desperate to escape it? But as he thought about it, he decided the idea did have a certain charm. Larry's new friend, Walter, was at the house on a regular basis. Matthew had met no one, so it was especially irritating to see them there every day in the same bedroom that he had shared with Larry for so many years. It would be good to come home after a long day and not deal with anyone or anything.

The house was full of memories of their living together, like the black and white 8 × 10 photos in the hall framed in non-reflective glass; one of Matthew standing in a wilderness of waist-high grass with a cocktail glass in his hand, and another, a profile of Larry peering into a box-turtle's shell. The pictures had been taken one summer afternoon when they went into the everglades with a basket of croissants, a block of cheese, and a bottle of white wine to watch the sun color the evening sky. Matthew stood with arms akimbo, looking at the bank of Palmetto silhouetted against a pink light, a ribbon of cloud separating the pink from the blue. A snowy egret sailed across the panorama unaware of them and the cry of an unseen animal came rhythmically from the Palmetto bank.

"If you listen closely to the sounds of the animals, and the woods, and the wind and the water," Matthew said to Larry, who was sitting on the checkered table cloth, "it's like a symphony. Every sound has its place and comes on cue."

"Why don't we break out the croissants," Larry said, and Matthew dropped down next to him wondering if his lover appreciated being alone together. Then he turned around, poured two glasses of wine, clinked Matthew's glass, and said, "To you, the best thing that ever happened to me." They nibbled cheese arm-in-arm and watched the egrets fly.

It would be nice to have a place that was just his and not his *and* Larry's. On the other hand he had never been alone. Which would be more devastating—the loneliness of an apartment, or dealing with Larry and his friend? He knew he could manage being at the house. He didn't know if he could handle being on his own. What if he couldn't? What if he moved into the apartment and couldn't take it? At worst, he could live with Carlos for a while. He had friends. He wouldn't suffer. A man's riches can be found in the devotion of his friends. They would be there if he couldn't handle it. They were always there. He began to read the classifieds and looked at hundreds of places that were too expensive or too big or too small. Then a friend told him of an opening in his building in a neighborhood off Biscayne Boulevard that had been innundated by Haitian refugees. The rent was more than reasonable, and the fact that there was someone upstairs that he knew, made it somehow right. Matthew paid the first and the last month's rent and moved in.

Carlos called for a meeting of the auxiliary to inspect the premises.

"It's a little bare," Matthew apologized, "but that's only because I don't have anything on the walls yet. I want to put a painting there. I don't like the carpet either, but I'll live with it."

"You could really fix this place up if you wanted to," John said, looking around with an artist's eye.

"A little paint can do wonders," Carlos agreed.

"I wanted to ask you about that. What do you think? Should I get some color in here?"

"Oh, definitely," Carlos jumped. "I think a nice rose would be just perfect. Change the whole feeling."

"I don't think I could take rose for very long."

"It sounds worse than it would look," John said.

"I was thinking of something a little more subtle," Matthew admitted. "Let the paintings stand out, you know?"

"I don't know how you can stand those bare walls," John said. "Maybe a large painting. I mean about five feet."

"You're really into big, aren't you?" Carlos said.

"The space calls for it," John argued.

Carlos turned to Matthew and said, "Sometimes I think he feigns innocence."

"That might work," Matthew responded to John.

"Sounds awfully traditional to me," Carlos complained. "What about lilac?"

"No. I tend to be traditional, anyway," Matthew said. "Actually, I don't even know how long I'm going to be here. I may want to find another place later on. There's even a possibility that I might be transferred to the West Coast."

"You're kidding." John said.

"It's only a possibility and a remote one at that."

"You may as well make it comfortable anyway," John reasoned.

"Larry and I still have the house up for sale, but we're not making a real effort to sell it either."

"That may take a while," John said from experience. "The house I sold in Lauderdale was on the market for more than a year."

"I know," the host said. "It doesn't matter, really. Maybe I can get a little house in the Grove."

"So you'll be getting something from the sale then," John said.

"Naturally. We'll divide the estate."

"When I left Brad, there was no settlement," John remembered. "No dividing of estate. We shared five years together, bought a house, and carefully guided its growth. But all I was really doing during that time was paying rent. It was never my house. It was his house, and I was allowed to remain in it for as long as I was his lover. And when that ended, I left with whatever was mine before we met and no more."

"We had a different type of arrangement," Matthew said. "Everything was communal."

"How do you know Brad and I didn't have a communal relationship?"

"We shared a joint bank account. We bought the house together."

"Divorce is such a nasty business," Carlos said.

"It's never pleasant," Matthew agreed.

"Actually we parted on good terms," John confessed.

"It's really the children that suffer," Carlos said, assuming a pensive air.

There was a pause, and Carlos asked, "So what's going on this weekend?" Then turning to John, "Are you and Bob going to be consummating your relationship again?"

"No, Bob's in Key West for about a week."

"Not again?"

"No, he isn't," Matthew interrupted. "I was talking to him at Karleman's Wednesday night."

"He's back?" John said, realizing how stupid he sounded.

"Yes. I was going to sneak out but he saw me. I always feel awkward when I talk to him."

"That's because you know he's a taken woman," Carlos said dramatically.

"Maybe." Matthew considered the possibility.

"But he was supposed to call as soon as he got back," John said.

"Maybe he needed more time," Matthew suggested.

"Sometimes you need a vacation from all the things that you have going on here at home, even if you don't go anywhere."

"That's true," John conceded. "But he was out at the bar."

"So. That's pleasure, not work," Matthew answered.

"And what am I, forced labor?"

Matthew laughed. "In a sense. Relationships are hard work."

"I'll say," Carlos added, rolling his eyes.

"Sometimes you need to stand back a little."

"Yeah, about 165 miles!" John said. He went to the window and looked out.

"Now stop reading into everything. If he didn't call, then call him if you feel the need."

"But he might need the space," John was becoming distraught. "You're right. I don't want to move in on him. That would only make things worse."

"All right. Then accept your decision," Matthew said. "Know that he'll call when he's ready and enjoy yourself in the meantime."

"That's right, honey," Carlos said. "We're gonna go out and show that place how to get down tonight." He let out a scream of joy. "I can feel it coming on now. Are we ready? ARE WE READY?" he repeated louder, like a cheerleader preparing the crowd.

"We're ready," Matthew said.

"We're ready," John joined.

They went to the bar and danced until three. Then John went out and had anonymous sex with a polite stranger.

Three days passed, and for three days the phone was silent. John thought that was enough time. He needed to be comforted. He needed answers, and he was feeling frustrated and angry. The more he thought about it, the more bizzare the circumstances became in his imagination, and the angrier he got. He determined not to let resentment get the best of him. He needed an outlet and the best way to quell the raging fire was to confront the issue directly, so, he summoned up his courage and called Bob. The phone rang. Unnerved he hoped Bob wasn't home.

"Hello."

"Bob? Hi, it's John."

"Oh, hi," Bob said brightly as though he were pleased. "How are you doing?"

"Fine," John said, trying to keep it light and friendly. "How was the trip?"

"Just great. It was so good to see Ron again. And I needed the vacation. Too many pressures at the hospital and all."

"Yes, I know. Well, you sound refreshed and ready to go again."

"I wish I had another week, actually."

"It always seems too short," John agreed.

"We were up most nights 'til two just sitting around talking. Catching up. I had to sleep on the couch, though. I didn't like that part. At least now I've got my own bed. Oh, I saw Matthew at the club the other night," Bob said, covering himself.

"Yeah, he goes there a lot. Neighborhood bar, I guess."

"I'm sorry I didn't call you sooner. I didn't mean for you to have to call me."

"What happened?"

"Well, I've been thinking about it, and I guess I kept putting it off because it was difficult for me, and time sort of slipped by."

John became annoyed at the casualness of the statement. "You know, this whole thing seems to be more of a difficulty for the both of us than it is a comfort." Despite his resolution to stay calm, he heard his voice rising. "I don't see any sense in us always being upset. Maybe it would be better if we called it off."

"That's a little drastic isn't it?"

"At this point I'm not so sure. I feel like you have to get away from me to catch your breath, like it's a real chore for you to see me, and I don't want this to be something you have to force yourself to do. I always thought you were supposed to feel good about a relationship, and that doesn't seem to be happening. We've both become a mass of nerves. Everytime I talk to Matthew and Carlos it's the same thing. I just think it would be better for both of us."

"What do you think they're gonna say at the 500 Club?"

"I don't know. I thought you were upset that they were jumping to conclusions about us in the first place. Now you won't have to worry."

"I wasn't worried. I didn't want them to force us into anything. I wanted it to come from us." There was a long silence. "Well," Bob continued, "I won't try to push the issue."

John thought, I'm sure you won't, but didn't say anything.

"I certainly don't want you to feel uncomfortable. Can I at least call you . . . see how you are?"

"If you do that then I'll always be wondering if you're going to call or when you're going to call. I think it would be better if we broke it off clean."

"I feel bad about this."

"I don't want you to feel bad. I only want to do the right thing. And I'm not even sure what that is right now, but I've got to do something, even if it's the wrong thing."

"All right," Bob said weakly, not knowing what to say to salvage the relationship or even if knowing the right words would change anything.

John felt a welling of emotion in his stomach, "I'm going to say good-bye now."

"Well, I hope I see you sometime," Bob said, seemingly reluctant to let go of the last thread of connection between them. "At the club or wherever."

"Me too," John said honestly. "Good-bye."

"Good-bye."

John sat staring at the phone for a long time. "I tried. I really did," he said as though he were still talking to Bob and then he started to cry.

During the days that followed he nurtured a sense of loss. All of the books and the poster that Bob had given him were stuffed away in the back of a closet. He needed to wait for time to restore his sense of control. Their absence seemed to help lessen the pain of separation. Constant reminders fueled despair, and it was always better, or at least easier, for John to break away completely until a certain amount of psychic healing had occurred. Then he could bring the books back out, rehang the poster, and begin to assimilate the experience.

But that time was not now. This was a time of retreat, a time when all of Bob's things were removed, to lie in wait for John's wounds to heal. He would know when the ritual was over, when he could feel secure enough to be reminded, when he could see Bob in a bar and not feel the need to run away. He envied those free spirits who could break away from lovers and still talk casually with them about a new receipe, or the Dolphins' victory over Los Angeles. He felt inadequate and knew that it was his own thoughts that kept him penned in, like a racing horse inside a fenced pasture. The horse might easily jump the fence if only he knew that he could.

Matthew had once told him that it's not the circumstances in life that cause us to suffer, as much as it is the way that we react to those circumstances. "Everybody has setbacks," he said. "We all face rejection at some point. We all feel unjustly accused and we all suffer loss. Some people simply react more emotionally than others. Let's face it. Experience is the mechanism by which we grow. But it's a lot easier for the people who say, 'so what' or 'that's life.' They don't emphasize pain. The point I'm trying to make is that you can learn to react better."

But retreat was John's reaction, and for him, it was effective, a means of stabilization, a way to assimilate feelings and needs without being influenced by the machinery of experience. And so all traces of his involvement with Bob were eliminated.

One evening during John's emotional convalescence, Matthew stopped by with a pint of honey vanilla ice cream made without sugar, which he knew John loved. Mary Martin was singing, "I'm Gonna Wash that Man Right Outa My Hair" on the stereo. John got out two dishes and scooped ice cream into them.

"I don't know what it is that causes me to fall in love with people who are still in love with their last lovers," John said, handing one of the bowls to Matthew as he tried to clarify his feelings. "Is this some kind of retribution that I have incurred for something I did wrong centuries ago? I mean, what am I supposed to do? How am I to handle these experiences? Will they continue to happen until I put my foot down and say, 'No, no more. I won't allow myself to be used in this way?' Is that it? Am I supposed to stand up for what is best for me? Or am I supposed to see that the relationship stays within the realm of friendship and that's it?"

He paced the room, dish in hand, as if by moving about he could find some answers. "This is great ice cream, but I don't think I can eat much of it."

"That's o.k."

"Is it designed to hone my ability to tell the difference between friendship and romance?" John continued his thought. "I mean, I'd like to know. I realize that everyone who is attractive to me can't be my lover. Maybe I should have stayed friends with him. I don't know. Maybe I do run away like Carlos says."

"It's not running away when you remove yourself from a non-productive situation," Matthew said deliberately.

"A non-productive situation," John stopped and repeated the phrase, robotlike. "I'm not recognizing non-productive situations."

"Why do you always blame yourself for these things?"

"I don't know, Matthew. I'm not blaming myself. I just want to know why this happens to me. This is not the first time. What am I doing wrong? I become involved too easily. That's it." He looked at his friend. "If I'd only gone along for the ride. If I didn't care what he was doing or who he was seeing."

"If you didn't love him?"

"I'm so confused," he said, as he sat next to Matthew.

"That's right. You're still too close to see the value in it yet. Things will clear up later and you'll be in a better place to evaluate it. Stop blaming yourself for everything and stop protecting Bob."

"I'm not protecting Bob," John's brow wrinkled.

"So far, all I've heard was that you did this wrong and that wrong. You never once talked about what he might have done to cause problems for you. This was not a one-sided situation, you know. Let's face it. Bob was having some trouble dealing with this too, and he's made as many decisions along the way as you have."

"But I'm the one who allowed myself to get involved."

"Yes, that's true, but you didn't know what you were getting involved in. Had all the cards been laid on the table up front you might have found yourself acting differently. You didn't know what was going on until you had already become involved with him."

"That still doesn't explain why this always happens to me."

"I think it's probably very common, that's all. There are a lot of people out there getting over relationships. I don't think it only happens to you."

"You don't?"

"No. I've met people who were in similar situations. I didn't fall in love with them, though."

"And I do, is that it?"

"No."

"Wait a minute. That's why I left you at Karleman's the first time I met you."

"That's right and look at our relationship. You knew right from the beginning what the situation was and you proceeded accordingly."

"So it's not me."

"Not entirely. You've assumed all of the blame, and you shouldn't."

"You don't think I'm running away from the situation when I say, 'no more.' I mean I have to look out for myself too."

"True."

"There's something in the sound of that."

"The sound of what?" Matthew wanted him to clarify what he was getting at.

"It's like I'm being real shallow when I say that, just because I can't have someone for a romantic affair, I don't want to be his friend. I think I separate my friendships from my romantic interests."

"I think most people separate their friendships from their romantic interests."

"Carlos doesn't."

"You want to be like Carlos?"

"I'm just saying that not everybody separates the two."

"I think he does. He just doesn't admit it."

"It sounds like I'm being real selfish."

"It may sound that way but you've got to look out for

yourself just like you said. Look at it from the other perspective. Bob is looking out for himself when he acknowledges that he's having difficulty. He had a relationship that ended, and he was testing the waters, so to speak, by going out with you, but he found that he wasn't ready yet so he made adjustments. Wasn't he the one who said that he needed more space?"

"Yes."

"That's looking out for himself. In the same way, you're acknowledging that you can't handle being his friend when it's a romantic involvement that you really want. Maybe things will change further down the line. I don't know. But right now," Matthew paused to let the 'now' sink in, "you're doing what's best for you. And I don't see anything wrong with that."

John took a deep breath and let it out. "I have to think about this some more." There was a pause, then John looked at his friend. "What are you smiling about?"

"You finished all your ice cream."

15.

On the day of Janet's wedding, the winter sun was waning below the horizon, painting the sky a spectacular shade of deep vermilion—brightest where it touched the earth. It resembled a fresco in a Renaissance cathedral. Long puffs of cloud were illuminated from below, their undersides luminously white and their tops a soft, dark silver. Where they stood the sky was striated with bands like the lines of a Van Gogh painting. Above the clouds was an iridescent blue, the kind of color that John wished he could put on canvas, but which was achieved only by light. Light, he thought, that inexplicable phenomenon upon which our perceptions rely, that force that all things were a part of and without which nothing exists. The word that exemplifies life and timeless knowledge even as its opposite was death and ignorance.

Below this radiant sky, the landscape was dotted with puddles of color in the drab green of twilight. Church spires and man-made towers, like the Biltmore Hotel, reached up to catch the last remaining beams of the sun. The red-tiled dome of the Church of the Little Flower in Coral Gables slowly gave up its light. The parking lot across the street was full, men in dark suits and women in pastel dresses were answering the call of the bells, walking toward the heavy double doors that opened into the anteroom of the sanctuary. John, Matthew, and Carlos were greeted at the door and asked if they were guests of the bride or the groom. They answered appropriately and were led through the black iron gates into the main hall. The interior of the church glowed, a dim unnatural yellow. Their heels clicked on the stone terrazzo floor of the wide center isle. The usher showed them a pew and they were seated on the left-hand side.

A strange feeling overcame John as he looked into the alcoves where the confessionals were located. He remembered his youth when he dreaded those boxes that his mother and father required him to enter. He recalled, too, how he had fretted as the time approached to tell the priest in the window about his impure thoughts and deeds. He hoped he would get the younger one who told him to say five Our Fathers and five Hail Marys so that he would be saved until the next time. But if the old priest was there, he would talk loud and want to know what those deeds were. John had to explain, and the old man cautioned him about the seriousness of his actions, whereupon John promised never to think such things again and left.

He thought of how at one point in his youth he was going to be a priest. That would have surely made his parents proud. They went to mass every Sunday even though they were forbidden to receive the Eucharist because his father had been previously divorced. Every week they sat quietly while the other members of the congregation wondered what sin they had committed that kept them from the altar. John wondered what power the church had over them that kept them coming to suffer the same humiliation week after week, year after year. What kind of control did it exercise that held them fast within its grip? He finally decided that it was the power of belief. They believed that the church was the only true way to salvation and because they believed it, its power was made binding.

He remembered the four of them sitting side by side in church one Sunday as the old priest read from the New Testament. "According to your faith, be it done unto you," he quoted and again he quoted, "As thou hast believed, so be it done unto thee." It was the same thing that Matthew had said about the nature of thoughts and beliefs. He wondered if his parents could have changed their belief that they were unworthy of the Eucharist. But they didn't have to—their belief was changed for them by Pope John, who decreed their crime to be forgivable, and what was once a deadly mortal sin at once became acceptable, which made them all the more devoted. They would have been proud to see their son ordained into the priesthood, but he decided to become an artist instead.

He could not wait for the church to change its mind about him. He reasoned that God was too universal, too complete to be restricted to one single religion and that the infinite could not possibly be contained in one finite book which, itself, had been changed from century to century. The light of God, he thought, was not present became of the candle which burned incessantly upon the altar but because of the light which was seated in his being. Thus he sat quietly contemplating amidst the resplendent trappings of the wealthiest religion on the earth.

As they waited for the ceremony to begin, John examined the vast expanse that stretched around and over him. Through the rear arch was the alcove that held the illuminated altar perched on seven steps. It was draped in white and surrounded by masses of brilliant white lilies. Two ornate Corinthian pillars rose up from behind on either side of a crucifix as part of an intricate gilded lattice work and supported a lintel inscribed in gold with the words EGO SUM LUX MUNDI: I am the light of the world.

The organist sat behind his instrument, which was piled up with electronic equipment and wires. He touched the recorder and a reel began to turn out the processional strains of Handel's "Largo" from *Xerxes*. Ladies in violet dresses began to appear. The congregation rose, and the groom made his way to the altar gate. The wedding parade had begun. They floated down the long center aisle holding candles to light the way. Janet made her appearance at the gates of the anteroom, clinging to the arm of her father, who was not necessarily pleased to be giving his daughter away outside the synagogue. But he wasn't strict with her. He wanted her to be happy and he knew that Anton could do that for his daughter and so he let her go. She was dressed in the most traditional of gowns with a long veil and a train that stretched far behind.

Watching Janet, John couldn't help remembering the years they huddled together in the office talking excitedly about the dates they had over the weekend. The stories piled up like chapters in an ever-unfolding book, the senator from D.C. who came down quarterly and took her to the most expensive restaurants; the baseball player who forgot to tell her about his wife; the drug dealer with the yacht who sailed her to Bimini and then told her he couldn't swim; the old art dealer who took her dancing at the Doral; the puppeteer who did shows in Palm Beach; they all flashed through his memory, along with the realization that there would be no more such figures to laugh and cry over. Like a father giving up his daughter, John felt a certain sadness that life would never be the same between them. Carlos and Matthew were his new confidants, the transfer was being completed. While one was taken away, two were put in its place. When Janet reached them and saw John out of the corner of her eye, she turned her head slightly and smiled at him, while at the same time trying to maintain a sense of decorum. At the gate she left her father for Anton's hand, and he escorted her to the altar where they stood together.

The church was silent as another thought began to take hold of John. While Janet was giving herself wholly to Anton, he had taken himself wholly away from Bob. He fantasized that things were different and that he was standing there on the altar steps with his beloved at his side. He indulged his daydream for only a short time before pulling himself back to reality. He felt lonelier than ever, and silently chastised himself for brooding. He looked over at Carlos standing next to him, and at Matthew, who was next to Carlos. Matthew looked into his eyes and knew his thoughts. He smiled gently and John smiled back. Carlos also knew instinctively what was transpiring. He leaned over to John and whispered words of encouragement. "We must maintain strength during times of trial and keep our minds fixed firmly upon the champagne orgy that is sure to follow."

The lights slowly dimmed again as the wheels on the tape deck began to turn. The low opening chords of the *Pachebel Canon* resounded through the hall. The bride and groom each took a candle and lit it from the ever-burning flame of the altar. Side by side, they descended the steps to the pews, where additional candles were supplied for each guest. The bride went to the first person on the left side of the hall, who happened to be her father, and lit the candle he was holding. Anton lit the candle of the first person on his side. The flame was passed down one by one until the whole church was aglow with the light of a hundred flames. It was in this fire-light that the ceremony of the rings was performed. No one had come forth in protest, as no one ever does. The pronouncement was made, and Janet and Anton were man and wife for ever and ever. Amen.

Though Janet and Anton had decided not to have children, that wasn't the case with John's brother Paul. He lived in Hollywood with the Puerto Rican girl named Rose, whom he married when John was in the South of France. They owned a two-bedroom house with cathedral ceilings and a microwave oven, had a van and a stationwagon (with a bumper sticker that read, "Crime Solution: God and Family"), and two kids.

Though as brothers they had shared their early lives together and entertained the same memories, their current existence was in no way similar. They moved, as if in different spatial dimensions—so much the same in their nature, so much removed in their manifestation. Paul was polite and tolerant but felt rather sad that his brother had missed out on all of the things that he felt were important like children, a wife, and a home in the suburbs. Things that television evangelists called "the backbone of America." John remained unaffected, since he saw no importance in any of those things, except perhaps, love. Their interests, their friends, and their experiences were to be as separate as the continents.

Yet there was something between them that went beyond all of the things that normally designated relationships between people. Something fragile and thin, of which both remained aware. Something set in bonds of the past. They rarely saw each other except on special occasions. They made plans on the phone and always ended by saying, "Yes, we'll have to do that," and then hung up, knowing that they never would.

One chilly January Sunday, not long after Janet's wedding, their paths came together. Paul had said that he was coming into Miami on business, and John suggested that he bring Rose along and stop over for coffee afterward. Paul eagerly agreed. They left the kids at Rose's mother's house that evening and headed south. Each time the three of them had been together, Rose had said how much she hated the city. "I don't know how you can stand to live down there. Everytime I go near the place I get paranoid. All you ever hear about on the news in refugees and crime. Every five minutes another boat is coming in. There's some nice houses up near us for sale. Why don't you think about coming to Hollywood. At least we'd be closer together."

But that would be like asking a dolphin to move to Denver. John loved Miami. Even as a boy before the onset of puberty, before he realized that a city had a sexual life, he loved to sit in the open window at his cousin's apartment on South Street and watch the yellow taxis go over the Brooklyn Bridge. Live in Hollywood? Impossible. Miami was infinitely more exciting, a city in the making. He had watched its development and growth from a transient community filled with people headed for someplace else to a world banking center and international trade market. Its identity, he felt, was still obscure and waiting to take form. John was a part of that growth, like Menes raising Memphis out of the desert sands.

John had spent hours arranging the apartment, the voice of Bette Midler urging him on. He cleaned and she sang,

> Fish may fly through the purple keys.
> Golden birds take to air . . .
> Only in Miami.

Every so often he would call out, "Sing it Bette." After side two had played three times, he put on the head phones so that the neighbors wouldn't think he was obsessive. He took the fish planter that his brother had given him last Christmas out of its hiding place in the kitchen and displayed it prominently in the living room near the window.

He wondered how the evening would go with Paul and Rose. It was always more difficult to talk to people who came to visit him (as opposed to the other way around) because they expected to be entertained. The burden of merriment was upon him.

It was eight-thirty and John began to grow impatient. Paul had said that they would be by a little after eight. John sat fidgeting in the high-backed chair that faced the couch and hoped that the coffee he made would still taste fresh when they got there. Waiting was the thing he hated most. When they finally arrived, he jumped off the chair, thought, "Thank God", and opened the door.

"Hello there," Paul said smiling.

"Hello there yourself," John responded.

"Hi," Rose said smoothly and offered her cheek.

"We got lost," Paul said.

"Oh, no," John pretended to be upset and pushed the door closed. "Course, if you came by more often, you wouldn't have that problem."

"Took us almost an hour," Paul complained.

"Did you follow my directions?"

"No, we came in from the other direction."

"Then you deserve to get lost. Only takes thirty-five minutes from here to your house."

"Next time we're going to fly," Rose said with a Mona Lisa smile.

"Where's the kids?"

"Rose's mother's. We dropped them off before we came."

"Oh."

"You have so many fragile things around," Rose said. "I'm afraid they'll turn the place over."

"Not much room in here," Paul said, looking up at the seven-foot ceiling.

"You got that right," John agreed.

Rose sat down on the couch and squinted, "Did you read all those books?"

"Most of them. Some I only got half-way through."

"Para . . ." she said slowly, like a child learning to read.

"Paracelsus."

"What's that?" she asked.

"Who. It's a person."

"He reads all this weird stuff," Paul said. "He once told me that they were hooking up plants to lie detectors in hopes of using them in court as witnesses. I mean that's weird."

"You know what they say," John reminded them. "Truth is stranger than fiction."

"Well," Paul said. "I've always thought you were truthful." Then he broke out laughing at his own pun.

John looked sympathetically at Rose, "You poor thing."

"You see how I suffer," she said, wide-eyed and dead serious. "Let me tell you, marriage has its ups and downs like everything else."

"I'm sorry to hear that," John said.

"Oh, how's Bob doing?" she asked.

John flushed and hoped it didn't show in the dim light. "He's alright." He hadn't told them about his breakup with Bob, preferring to remain instead an image of stability in their eyes. He didn't want his brother to think that homosexuals were incapable of lasting relationships. He set himself up to be the shinning example of all gay people, and was determined to influence the opinion of the straight world by making sure that his family thought well of him. He had cultivated this image ever since Anita Bryant began her dark campaign back in 1977.

"Why is it you've never brought Bob over for dinner?" Rose asked.

"Well, he's busy," John answered. "I hardly ever know what his schedule is."

"We never had that problem when we were dating, did we?" she asked her husband.

"Yes, we did," Paul argued. "You were working nights and I was on days." John was thankful that the conversation was drifting away from talk of Bob.

"Oh, that's right. We did, didn't we."

John excused himself and went to the bathroom. He stood streaming into the bowl and examining his face in the mirror that covered the wall over the sink and the commode. Paul sat looking through the record collection next to the couch, while Rose put her head back against a cushion and stared at the ceiling. There was a faint rapping at the front door. Paul got up, turned the knob, and gingerly pulled it open. Carlos stood in the porch light with eyes closed, nose turned up, and one arm positioned dramatically against the wall. He was wearing long white gloves that came to his elbows and red high heels. "Well," he said into the night, "how do I look?"

When Paul didn't answer, Carlos opened his eyes. The expression of horror on Paul's face suggested that he had the wrong apartment and Carlos nonchalantly checked the number next to the door. It was the right address. "Is John home?" he asked cooly, releasing the wall.

Rose was leaning over the side of the couch looking out the door beneath her husband's arm. "Ah . . . yes," Paul said. "Come on in."

"Thank you," Carlos floated in. "I don't always dress like this."

John's eyes widened in the mirror to twice their size when he heard Carlos' voice saying that he didn't always dress like this.

"You must be Bob," Rose said, demonstrating her acceptance through familiarity.

"Heavens no!" Carlos exclaimed, taking off his hand wear and sitting down. John came rushing out of the bathroom barely zipped, expecting the worst and seeing it.

"Carlos!" he said exasperated. "What are you doing here?"

"I didn't know you had company," Carlos apologized; then he grimaced at the floor, "They thought I was Bob, of all people."

John let out his breath and did the only thing he could. "This is my brother, Paul and his wife, Rose." He went through the amenities.

"Pleased to meet you," Carlos politely nodded in their direction.

"This," John proclaimed, "is my friend, Carlos. We've

known each other for . . ." A shock ran through him. "What is that on your feet?"

"Oh, these," Carlos pointed one foot into the air and turned it around at the ankle. "I picked them up at a church bazaar in the Roads. Aren't they divine?"

"I'm glad I didn't see them first," Rose said affectionately, leaning forward. "I would have fought you for them."

"Oh, they would look great on you," Carlos shreiked, throwing his hands into the air. Paul looked on in astonishment as the two of them broke into immediate chatter like two ladies at a bazaar.

John felt relieved that Carlos and Rose were getting along, even though he noticed that his own behavior from that point on was slightly more masculine as if to compensate for Carlos' affectation.

"How's the van running?" John asked his brother.

"Like a charm," Paul said.

"Oh, is that your van outside?" Carlos asked.

"Um-hmm," Paul nodded.

"I love the artwork."

"How did you see that?" John asked. "It's dark out."

"It's parked right under the street light," Carlos answered. "I'm undecided about the purple stripe though."

"We hooked up a little generator in it, so we'll have electricity when we take it out," Rose said.

"All the comforts of home," John commented, trying to keep this innocent line of conversation going.

"I don't suppose you've ever gone camping?" Paul asked Carlos.

"Oh, are you kidding?" Carlos said. "I do it all the time."

"Is that right?" Paul started to warm toward him a little.

John fidgeted in his chair. "Would anybody like some coffee," he asked desperately.

"I'll have a little," Rose said.

"Me too," Carlos said, and John felt his last hope for a smooth evening slip away. Defeated, he went into the kitchen.

"We just came back from a trip to the West Coast. Bonita Springs. Not far from Fort Myers," Paul told Carlos.

"Oh, that's nice," he responded.

"Where have you gone recently?"

"Pardon me?"

"Camping."

"Oh, just everywhere. You name it. I've camped there."

"Ouch. Damn it," came a cry from the kitchen.

"You need some help?" Rose called out.

"No. It's all right. I just spilled some coffee on my arm."

"Have you been to Blue Ridge?" Paul seriously asked the slender man in high heels.

"No, I don't think so."

"West Coast?"

"No."

"Keys, then?"

"Absolutely."

"Oh," Paul turned to his wife, "we went to the Keys last year, right?"

"We have some friends who own land on Key Largo," Rose said, "so we park the van there and rough it."

"Yeah," Paul continued, "it's really nice. Right on the water and no one else around."

John returned with a tray of full cups and put them down on the coffee table.

"John, you met Liz and Mike next door, didn't you?" Paul asked.

"Oh, yeah, sure."

"I was telling Carlos how they let us camp out on their land down in Key Largo."

"Sounds great."

"You know what I like best about it," Paul smiled mischievously, putting a hand on Rose's knee.

"What's that?" his brother asked.

"Making love out in the wild with the stars overhead. You get a real sense of freedom."

"You don't have to tell me," Carlos said. "I know exactly what you mean."

"It just seems so natural, you know, out in the wild where we first came from. No walls, no traffic, just the leaves, and the grass, and the water lapping up against the shore."

"You would love Virginia Beach," Carlos turned to John, "Wouldn't he?"

"No, I don't think so."

"What's at Virginia Beach?" Paul was curious.

"Nothing you'd be interested in," John shrank.

"Oh, stop," Carlos intervened. "Tell him."

"Tell me," Paul begged.

"It's a natural beach with woods that come right down to the shore. Sort of like the Keys. They haven't touched it yet."

"That's not the part he wants to know about."

"Carlos!" John was irritated.

"What?" Paul asked thinking he might lose the tip.

"They have a nude beach where the bushes are just abuzz with love in the wild, as you so beautifully put it," Carlos said and John rubbed his moustache nervously.

"Do they have a camp grounds there?" Paul asked.

"No," Carlos said. "Just love in the wild."

"Is it just guys?" Rose asked. John was surprised at how well they were handling this.

"Depends on where you go," Carlos said. "You two could have a ball."

"I didn't think there were any natural beaches left in Miami," Paul said.

"It's just a matter of time." John seized the first chance to steer the conversation to more mundane areas.

"Right," Paul said. "That's why we take off. There's only one problem with being out in the woods."

"What's that?" John asked.

"No football."

"Good," Rose said. "As far as I'm concerned that's a blessing."

"Oh," John asked his brother. "Did you watch the game last week?"

"Of course. I had fifty dollars riding on it."

"I take it you were rooting for the Hurricanes," John said confidently.

"Naturally," Paul said, feeling more comfortable now that they were safely off the beach, "I never liked Nebraska anyway, even if they are the best in the country."

"They WERE the best in the country," John said. "You should have come down here. I've never seen a town go crazy like this one did that night. It was more than two teams playing a game. It was two cities battling for a title."

"You have no idea what it's like to be a football widow," Rose confided to Carlos.

"Yes, I do, dear," he said leaning forward, legs crossed. "Randy, my ex, was addicted to the thing. I mean, come Sunday afternoon, I knew just where to find him."

"You really do understand," Rose was delighted. "Good, let them talk about sports. I can't get over your shoes. I simply love them."

16.

Wednesday afternoons at work were always reserved for staff meetings which took place in the ninth floor conference room. John hated being boxed up in a room with fourteen executives, listening to the boss drone on about the things they needed to do and weren't doing. The head secretary complained about scratchy handwriting and about everyone forgetting to tell her their whereabouts in case she needed to reach them. In addition, she made her usual overstated speech about time sheets and their "utmost importance." John usually sat quietly in the corner with the other artist and the two photographers, who made the hour almost bearable. When it was over, he was the first to leave. He stepped out of the elevator and entered the small reception area. "Hi Gloria," he said to the small blonde woman with big round glasses sitting at the desk.

"Hello John. How was the meeting?"

"A real treat! You know how much I like them."

"Yes. I wish I could have been there," she said in her West Virginia drawl.

"You're just lucky, I guess."

"Oh, there's a message for you. I put it on your phone."

"Business or pleasure?"

"I don't know, couldn't tell."

"Male or female?"

"Male."

"Oh, good, a glimmer of hope for the weekend." He started down the hall.

"By the way, Mr. Bucchi."

He turned back, "Yes?"

"I don't think I have your fifty cents for Marsha's birthday doughnuts." She put out her hand and flapped her fingers against an open palm. "Cough up."

"My God, every time I see this woman she's asking me for money."

"Oh, come on. It's for a good cause."

"Sending our head writer into a hypoglycemic fit is a good cause? You do have a morbid streak, don't you."

"We'll buy diet doughnuts. Fifty cents please."

John reached down into his pocket for the cash. "One of these days you're gonna break me, you know that?"

"You'll just have to postpone the Porsche for another month, that's all I can say."

"Here."

"Thank you, John."

"You know," he said. "I think you're all right. I don't care what the others say."

"Get out of here."

He dashed away down the hall that wound around to his office. A small square sheet of paper stuck behind the outer edge of the dial. He rolled out his chair, sat down, and picked up the message. A shock went through his body as he read MR. BOB ANGSTROM. Two boxes were checked off, 'called', and 'please call.'

He hadn't seen or heard from Bob in months. He had avoided going to the places that he knew Bob frequented. Once, though, he had gone to Karleman's with Matthew and Carlos, and Bob had walked in. A man that John was standing next to had actually asked if he was all right because his face had changed expression so dramatically. (His emotions were always easily visible in his face.) Bob stopped to say hello but the meeting was awkward. He kissed Matthew and Carlos as usual, but refrained from any demonstration of affection toward John, who veiled his discomfort by keeping time to the music. John took the first opportunity to leave, knowing that Bob was aware of his swift departure. That was the last time John had been to Karleman's on the weekend. He lived as a fugitive, always in retreat.

He flinched and stared at the paper for several minutes. His eyes circled the office, looking at the poster, then at the small drawing by Janet of a laughing green dragon, before returning to the phone. Suddenly, he moved as if someone had thrown a switch. He picked up the receiver and dialed the number.

"Hello," the familiar voice said.

"Hello, Matthew? It's John."

"I was thinking about you. What's up?"

"I just got a message from Bob."

"Oh, really. What did he want?"

"I don't know. I was in a meeting and found a note that he called me. What am I gonna do, Matthew?"

"I expect you'll call him back."

"Why is he calling me?" John moaned. "I thought it was over. Why is he calling if it's over?"

"Now calm down. I don't know why he's calling but don't make it into something it isn't. He probably wants to see how you are or say hello. It's no big deal."

"I'm blowing this out of proportion again, aren't I?"

"I think you are a little bit. But that's all right. At least you realize it, and now you can start to think of it in its proper place."

"I can't believe I'm still reacting like this."

"It's only natural. I mean it was an unexpected shock to see the message, but I'm glad you called."

"Matthew, I don't know what I'd do without you."

"Are you going to call Bob?"

"I should, but I'm really nervous about it."

"Well, he's probably expecting to hear from you. If you don't call, he'll think you don't want to talk to him anymore. He probably won't call you back. It's your decision."

"I know. It's not that I don't want to."

"It's hard. I'm not saying it isn't, but he's made an effort here. Are you going to respond to that?"

"I guess so. I owe him that much."

"Good."

"I'll talk to you later, Matthew. I'm gonna call now."

"Okay. Good luck."

He wondered why Matthew had said "good luck". He wasn't gambling; he wasn't going to ask anything of Bob in hopes of a positive response, he was only responding to a call. He pressed the receiver button, took a deep breath, and dialed again. He held the last number against the finger stop for a moment before letting it go. The secretary asked for his name and said, "Just a minute, please."

"Hello, John," the voice came on bright and cheerful.

"Hello, Bob. How are you doing?"

"Oh, fine. It's good to hear your voice again. I was talking with Rick about you the other day and wondered how you were."

"Everything is going along pretty well." He was much calmer than he thought he would be. "Are you still as busy as ever?"

"It never stops."

"I know what you mean."

"As a matter of fact, that's one of the reasons I had called."

"What's that?" John said, wondering what was about to be dropped.

"Well, the 500 Club is doing a benefit show next month, and we need to have some brochures done up, and I was wondering if you'd be interested in helping us with that since you're so talented in that area. I figured you would be the one to contact."

John thought, *So that's why he's calling me, he wants a favor.*

"Well," he said, "I'm not really doing any freelance work right now because I'm swamped here, and they kind of frown upon us doing anything like that. Do you have any alternate plans? I hate to be the one to mess you up."

"Oh, yeah, no problem. I thought I'd call you first because you do that kind of thing, but I can get someone at the club to do it. Besides, I just wanted an excuse to call you anyway. God, it's been so long since we talked."

"I know," John softened. Bob hadn't called him about business, after all.

"What have you been doing with yourself?" Bob probed. "You don't go to Karleman's any more, do you?"

"Not a whole lot."

"Oh," Bob seemed about to ask why but didn't.

"I've started a new drawing that I'm really excited about."

"What is it, I mean, is it going to be a painting?" Bob seemed eager to keep the conversation going.

"No, it's pen and ink. I'm calling it "Transcendence." It's all little dots and lines. Gonna take a long time to finish, I think."

"I bet. Sounds great, though. Maybe you can get it published somewhere. There are always people looking for covers. Maybe we can use it for the program." Bob said, laughing.

John chuckled with him. "I don't think it's that kind of a picture."

"No, I know. I'm just kidding."

"Are you still at the house?"

"No," he said excitedly. "I finally sold it."

"No kidding." John's perception was immediately shifted.

"Yes. To tell the truth, I was really glad to get rid of it."

"I know it was a real problem for you."

"It was. So now I have an apartment not far from Jackson. I can walk to work. It's nice. There's a pool and a big yard that all the apartments are clustered around and the landlady is a crazy woman with eight cats."

"Well, at least you'll never be lonely."

"A lot of people from Jackson live there. I know half the residents."

"Well, I'm glad everything worked out. I guess I'd better get going."

"Yes, I'd better hang up too. Listen, take care of yourself, John." There was a pause. "I still think about you a lot, and it was good to talk to you."

"You too, Bob," he said, keeping in mind that he was talking to a friend and not a lover. "I'll talk to you again."

"Okay. Take care."

"Bye," John said and hung up the phone.

For a long while, he sat in the empty office. It was after five, and everybody else in the department had gone home. The silence was oppressive. No phones, no typewriters, no bosses screaming across the hall, no one shuffling by the open door. Quiet. Like the quiet of guns after a cease fire. A sense of well-being settled in him for no apparent reason. He thought about Bob for a minute and the conversation they had just shared. Both had chosen their words carefully, the language was strictly surface yet their feelings showed through the facade, evident in the tone of their voices. He gathered his things together and headed for the elevator.

Buses and taxis and cars and people crowded the street as everyone rushed to get home. He saw Janet and said goodnight as she headed toward the parking lot. He had left his car at the repair shop for new brakes that morning, so he walked to the train station above Government Center and joined the hordes of commuters on the southbound to Coral

Gables. He cursed as he glided up the escalator and heard the train leave above him, knowing that he'd have to wait another fifteen minutes for the next one.

A half hour later he was walking beneath the orchid canopy of Sidonia Avenue. He walked up to the pink building near the end of the block, turned the key in his apartment door, and went in, heaving a sigh in the stillness. He threw his clothes off, went over and opened the closet door. He pulled down a hanger, slipped his folded pants through them, and put them back on the rack. He stopped for a moment and stood there with his hand still on the clothes rack as if in a trance. Slowly, he moved his hands up to the shelf and closed his fingers around the books that Bob had given him. He pulled them down, looked at them, and passed his hands gently over their covers as if he could read them entirely by touch. Then he walked into the living area and made room for them on the book shelf.

17.

The sun moved up from the southern hemisphere shedding a new angle of light on the verdent earth below. As it crossed the equatorial line it marked the beginning of spring— a time of renewal when the days were longer. In times gone by it was the beginning of a new cycle, a new year in the old calendar, the first day of Aries, the first sign of the Zodiac. The new year now started on a date seemingly picked at random. It was not really the beginning of anything. No celestial event marked its onset. It started nine days into the beginning of the fourth seasonal change, in the cold dead of winter. And anyone back then who did not conform to the new random date and continued to celebrate the new year, as had been the custom, on the first day of spring was chastised and called an April Fool.

Carlos and Matthew sat in John's apartment surrounded by paintings, books, antiques, and plants. The upright piano had been sold when he moved from the larger apartment, but the stacks of sheet music sat on a shelf, waiting until times were better. Every space was used to its fullest. The seven-foot sofa barely fit against the wall under the window and came right up to the edge of the front door. An open-backed cypress shelf-unit occupied the west wall that had been covered with a smoked mirror. The tiny lights of the stereo reflected back from the mirrored wall and softly set the shelves aglow. The C Major crescendo of *Also Sprach Zarathustra* had built to an inspiring climax, and then stopped abruptly, leaving only a single low C chord to reverberate in the aftermath. The earth had been created. Strauss would take the piece through the advent of man and science and the eventual emergence of the Superman, a being who had learned to control his emotions and his passions. A being who would awake from his slumber of ignorance and dependence to live in the light of an illuminated mind, complete in himself.

John had made a pot of coffee, and they sat in the dim light that shone from behind a palm in the corner throwing pointed shadows across the low white ceiling.

"How long have we known each other now?" Matthew asked.

"It's been about a year, I guess," Carlos said. "No, actually I knew you a month longer than John because we both met him at Charlie's party."

"That's right."

"I have to tell you," John said. "This has been one hell of a year for me."

"You can count me in on that too," Matthew said.

"I mean I feel like I've really come a long way," John continued. "All those nights looking for someone to make me happy. I don't need someone else to make me happy."

"The name of the game is 'approval,'" Carlos offered. "And if YOU don't approve, nobody else is going to either."

"Out of the mouths of babes!" Matthew said.

"You know what I keep thinking," Carlos asked but didn't wait for anyone to respond, "It's sort of like being away at boarding school, the three of us, and we're all working on these lessons. You know, like fate pushed us together because each one of us had something the other needed."

"Ah," Matthew mocked. "The old life-is-a-school-room theory."

"I just wish we could stop having so many lessons,"

Carlos said. "I'm sick of lessons. I want to do some easy living for a change, you know. Don't we ever get a recess?"

"You get recess after you pass the test," Matthew said.

Carlos sighed, "That's what I was afraid of."

"It's interesting," John said, wondering if his friends would be able to understand the depth of his statement or if they would perceive him as the pretentious fool he hoped he was not. "Minds like Emerson, Gibran, and Hesse, all seem to be saying the same thing—that there's a greater existance, that what we like, the way we present ourselves, and even our sexual preferences are really of little consequence. The differences between people are all meaningless. It's only the things that are basic and shared by all of humanity that have any real significance at all."

"Well, that's what I've been saying to you all along," Matthew agreed. "The ways in which we are alike are more important than the ways in which we are not."

"Just think," John said. "There are those who go around moralizing and worrying about things that don't even matter. I mean some people spend their whole lives worrying about things that don't matter!"

The books from which he quoted sat on a shelf area next to the wall unit that reached from the floor to the ceiling. There were books on art, philosophy, metaphysics, literature, health, and travel. The books that Bob had given him were prominently displayed there.

"Truer words were never spoken," Carlos affirmed, raising a coffee cup delicately to his lips. "I mean, if we're going to worry, let's worry about something meaningful like why you don't have any saucers. Quite frankly, I don't care about the opinions of other people but all the world knows the importance of learning to entertain properly."

"It really has been a significant year, though," Matthew said. "I can't believe I'm finally living on my own. A first—

time event, mind you. If you had told me I'd be in my own apartment two years ago, I'd have said you were crazy."

"Matter of perspective," Carlos said.

"But I *am* on my own. I'm independent. Like John said, I feel good about myself and who knows what's ahead. I mean, if the I.R.S. decides they're going to offer me the transfer to the West Coast," he paused, "I think I'm going to take it. I can't believe I'm saying that. I'm the one who was scared to live alone if you recall."

"I recall we had to get you out of Larry's house with a crow bar," Carlos said, looking down his shoulder.

"Don't go to San Francisco," John said. "The land moves around out there; besides, your friends are here."

"I'm not worried about earthquakes and if the opportunity comes up, I am going to take it, even though I'll miss you. I think it would be good for me."

"Spoken like a real trouper," John said, embarrassed for trying to hold him back.

"And another thing," Matthew continued, "I don't think you guys realize the impact you've had on me—are still having on me. I don't mean to put it in the past tense. But I haven't usually been this open with people before. Now, all of a sudden, I'm chewing your ears off."

"You can nibble on my ear any time," Carlos said. "And it wasn't all of a sudden, believe me. To think of how I had to plot and scheme to find out what happened in the back of the Village Pub that night with Vic Ramona. I swear, getting information out of you has not been easy."

"I'll admit it took time for me to feel comfortable talking to you about certain things."

"Any things," Carlos emphasized.

"But that's what's so great about all of this," John said. "We can sit around and actually talk about things that are vital. I couldn't do that before I met you." John gazed with pleasure at his friends. "I've learned how really important it is for me to put feelings and thoughts into words—to categorize and speak them out loud to someone outside of myself. I mean I've thought some really strange things in my day."

"As we all know," Carlos agreed.

"But when I tell you about them, it sounds dumb and I figure it's not really that big of a problem after all. To carry them alone is not only difficult, it's unnecessary. The more I speak of my problems, the less I have to."

"Yes, but we're not used to talking about our feelings. At least I'm not," Matthew said. "That was a real concern of mine, I want you to know. At least now if I say something, I'm not going to worry that you'll like me any less."

"I didn't know you worried about that." Carlos was amazed.

"I felt that I had to keep this image. I had to be this perfect human being and I'm not perfect. But that's okay." Matthew spoke calmly and all three of them knew that he was not the same person he had been a year ago. He had gained, not only his independence, but a certain ease in the presence of others that comes only with a true sense of self.

"Of course it is, darling. There's nothing at all like the love between friends. The kind of love where you can fart out loud and still be wanted. It surpasses everything we know, and I dare say it is even more wonderful than money."

"I never thought you'd rate anything more wonderful than money," Matthew teased.

"Well, I *do*," Carlos said, emphasizing the last word.

"I can't imagine going through everything that happened with Bob and not being able to talk it out with you guys. I probably wouldn't have handled it very well."

"Sure you would," Matthew said. "You would have been a nervous wreck, that's all."

"I'll say. But I got a lot from him. I don't even know that I could put it into words."

"Love transforms," Matthew said.

"It does," John agreed.

"Did you ever tell him that you loved him?" Carlos asked.

"Not in so many words," John said thoughtfully.

Carlos leaned back. "You should have. Even if he didn't feel the same. I told Randy, and believe me, I know it isn't easy. But I'm glad the man at least knew. It would be a shame to let such a beautiful sentiment go unrevealed, like a diamond buried in the dirt. Do you think you'll ever tell him?"

"I doubt it," John said. "I don't think there's much sense in it at this point. I rarely see him anymore, and when I do it's all right. I don't go running for the door like I used to. It's comfortable now, and I'm not sure I want to drag out those old feelings again. He's over it. I'm over it."

"But there's always that special feeling that you have for them," Carlos said. Then he changed his tone. "But it's true. I never see Randy."

"I haven't seen Bob in months."

"I have no desire to see Larry."

"The gods are merciful once they've run us through," Carlos said pensively. "But I don't think I really wanted a lover to begin with. I was doing what I thought I was supposed to be doing. I felt that I wasn't settled down like my mother was."

"Are you doing what you want to be doing now?" John asked.

"Let's just say I'm content with what I'm doing."

"You don't feel that compulsion," Matthew said, "to find a mate right now, and live up to an unrealistic ideal."

"Right," John said. "That would be nice, of course, but you don't need it in order to feel that you have a purpose. I'm worth being loved even if nobody loves me."

"But people do love you," Matthew said.

"Yes, I know that," he smiled. "What I want to say is that even if you weren't here, I'd still love me."

"A little narcissism never hurt anybody," Carlos said very matter of factly. "Why, in elementary school I once voted for myself in a secret ballot for bathroom monitor."

"Did you win?"

"Out of a class of thirty-two, I received twenty-eight votes. There are some things you just can't keep secret. Why wasn't I born butch instead of brilliant?"

"Carlos, you wouldn't be the same," Matthew said.

"Oh, to be sure. When one is butch, one doesn't wear Van Cleef."

Matthew pushed him, and Carlos obligingly fell over on the couch.

EPILOGUE

It had been almost a year since that evening when the three of them gathered in John's apartment. And at the time it was only natural for them to assume that their friendship would go on forever. There was great comfort in looking into the future and knowing that, whatever happened, they would be able to call on each other for support, that there would always be a confirmation that whatever it was they were going through, really wasn't that bad. But permanence is never the way of things and the best of friends eventually separate, if not by choice, then by circumstance. Yet even though the physical encounters fall away, there is always a part of the other person that is absorbed. No one is ever left the same. And no one is ever himself alone, but becomes the bits and pieces of all of the people he has known throughout his life.

Matthew's boss at the I.R.S. gave him the chance to apply for the position in San Francisco and he went West to investigate. A friend of his, whom John and Carlos also saw at the bars occasionally, had already moved there and offered his place to Matthew for the week. John took him to the airport and saw him off. Matthew stayed for five days while he was interviewed. He impressed the company with his memory and his calm, down-to-earth approach. One week later he received a call from the personnel director in Miami saying that the transfer had gone through and that he should report to work in California in three weeks. Those three weeks were, for Matthew, the most difficult and the most exciting of his life. There were things to do, details to remember. He gave his landlady notice that she wouldn't be receiving a check next month. He gathered boxes to pack dishes, tools, records, books; all of the countless other things one collects over the years. Larry had him over for dinner and said that life would not be the same. John went to visit more than usual, knowing that these would be their "last" moments. One night the two of them were sitting on boxes and looking at the once again bare apartment when Matthew said, "Just think, now you'll be able to come out to San Francisco whenever you want."

"Right," John played along. "And, of course, you'll always have a place to visit here in Miami. We'll set up a coast-to-coast network." John suddenly became serious. "Damn, I'm going to miss you."

Matthew put his arms around him, and they held on to each other in silence. It was probably in that moment that they both knew that an era in their lives had ended. No matter how many vacations were spent, it would not be the same as when they shared their souls in the thick tropic night. But even in ending, there is a desire to hold on, to continue after the union has outlived its usefulness, a sadness in giving up someone who has been so instrumental and so much a part of life. At 6:30 on a brisk Monday morning, Matthew drove his packed station wagon out of Miami.

The past year had been a time of change for the three of them. Carlos had become involved in est training, and for him everything was 'perfect.' He went to seminars on Wednesday nights and developed a new set of relationships. These were the catalyst that helped to dissolve the old relationships but which one day themselves would be dissolved in the light of other newer experiences. John and Matthew had rarely seen him, except at the gala parties he threw, to which the two of them always received a printed invitation in the mail. The most recent before Matthew's departure had been the "Elegant Hearts" party during the first part of February. It offered a rare and eclectic collection of government officials, designers, bureaucrats, artists, men in leather, and girls in evening dress. During that evening, future parties were planned, deals were made, and lovers were found. Matthew's departure and eminent success was formally announced.

Carlos' mother was there that night, and John greeted her with smiles, saying, "I've met you before. I think it was at your daughter's house in Miami Lakes," and she responded by saying, "Oh, no it wasn't. It was in that bar in Coconut Grove." And John blushed. Part of Carlos' new training dealt with honesty, and in a bold gesture to reveal himself to his mother, he simply took her to a gay bar, thinking that there was nothing more convincing than first-hand experience. That was a night to be remembered, a night that Carlos would relate many times in the years to come.

They had gone to Hattie's and sat at the bar on tall stools. Mrs. Montana looked around at the furnishings as she settled in.

"Isn't this nice?" Carlos asked, as confidently as ever.

"It certainly is . . . pink, isn't it?"

He ordered two glasses of wine from the girl behind the counter, the same that served Matthew his Moosehead that memorable night the three of them had gone to the theatre.

"I notice that there are a lot of . . . unusual people in here tonight." Mrs. Montana said, looking about.

"I don't think they're so unusual."

"You don't?"

"No," Carlos said. "Everyone is well behaved and friendly."

"Yes. Friendly." She noticed the two lovers on the other side of the bar.

"Does it bother you, mother?"

"Well, I'm just wondering why you brought me here."

"I guess I wanted you to see my friends, and where I go.

It's all a part of me. I want to be honest with you, Mother. I want you to know ME."

"I see."

"Are you upset?"

"No, I wouldn't say that."

"Then what? Tell me. I really want to know."

"Actually, Carlos, this is not such a big surprise," she admitted.

"What do you mean, it's not a big surprise?" He raised his eyebrows, surprised himself.

"Well, it isn't."

He climbed down off the high stool and looked at her intently. "What are you trying to tell me, Mother?"

"Now, Carlos. Settle down."

He took his position on the stool again.

"Popi and I have always known that you were, well . . . colorful."

"Colorful?" he repeated rather loudly.

"Ssshhh," she frowned. "You're making this very difficult for me."

"I don't believe this!" he looked away and pouted with his chin against his fist. They didn't talk for at least a minute. That's when the burly woman, who was leaning against the wall guzzling a beer, walked over to Mrs. Montana. "Hi there, pumpkin," she said with one hefty nod.

"Pardon me?" Mrs. Montana looked up in surprise.

"Will you excuse us, please," Carlos swung around and said in a huff. "My mother and I are trying to talk."

"Sorry," the woman said sarcastically and walked back to the wall, mumbling something about how hard it was to get a good baby sitter.

"I still don't understand why you had to bring me here," Mrs. Montana said to her son. "A simple explanation would have been enough."

He chuckled under his breath. "I didn't think you'd

believe me. I figured that when you saw how nice everybody was, you wouldn't feel so bad."

"Some are nice. Some are a little too pushy, if you ask me," she glanced briefly over toward the wall.

"How long have you known about this?"

"Oh, I don't know, Carlos. A long time. You didn't want guns and trucks when you were little. You wanted a tea set, remember?"

"What about Popi?"

"No. Never. We never discussed it, your father and I."

"It doesn't bother you?"

"What can I do?"

"You can tell me it's all right."

"I can't do that. You do what you think is right, Carlos. I raised you the best I could. Now you're on your own."

There was a long pause as Carlos considered what his mother had said. It was broken when John walked in the door. "Carlos," he said, not seeing the woman at his side. "How you doing?"

"Hi, John," Carlos said mildly. "I've told you about John," he said, putting his hand on her back. He looked back up again. "I'd like you to meet my mother."

"Oh," John was stunned. Then he put out his hand, "It's nice to meet you."

She took it, smiled, and nodded, "My son feels that I need an education, John."

"This is her first time here," Carlos clarified.

"Well, I hope you're enjoying yourself."

"It's very nice."

"Well," John said again and looked about the room as if there might be something to say pasted on a wall somewhere. "Did you two go out tonight?" He made the effort and put his hands in his pockets.

"No," Carlos said. "Just here and we're about to leave."

"I wish I'd come in sooner," John lied.

"It was nice meeting you, John," she said, getting off the stool.

"You too," he answered, still in shock.

"I'll call you later," Carlos said and took his mother home.

Like Carlos, John also stayed in town even though he was the one who always talked about going back to New York and, in fact, had given Matthew the idea of leaving.

One night, not long after his friend's departure, John had gone back to Karleman's and stood in the corner a little too long before deciding that it was time to go home. He checked his pocket for his key and started to weave through the bodies. As he approached the front door, it opened and Bob appeared. John flinched but did not break his stride. He was calm and unaffected. Bob saw him, smiled, and walked in his direction.

"Hello, Bob," he said softly.

"John. It's good to see you again," he paused. "It's been a long time, hasn't it?"

"Almost a year."

"It doesn't seem that long."

"You get involved with different things," John said. "Time goes by."

"You're looking good."

"So are you. But then you always were a handsome devil."

He laughed and pulled John up against him and held him close for a minute. "Are you leaving already?" he said loosening his hold on John.

"Yes. I've been here long enough. It's time for a change."

"Aaah," Bob complained. "I just got here."

"Can you walk me out to my car?"

"Sure."

The door man opened the door for them and said, "Good night, gentlemen." The night sky was deep indigo. The stars were brilliant. Even with the traffic along Biscayne Boulevard, the parking lot seemed somehow peaceful, set apart, like the inside of a church before the celebration of the Eucharist.

"You know," John was able to begin as they reached his car. "There's something I never got the chance to tell you."

"What's that?" he said anxiously.

"I never got to tell you how much our time together meant to me." He searched Bob's eyes. "And I don't want you to say anything to this or feel the need to respond. I want to state a fact and leave it at that."

"All right."

"I don't know what it is that makes people drift apart or why we do the things we do, but I want you to know that, ah . . . well, I guess what I'm trying to say is . . . those feelings that I had for you, they weren't surface feelings. I know you find it hard to believe that something like love can happen in so short a time. And maybe you're right. But, you were a turning point for me. No . . . don't say anything. Just let me finish, please. It would be a shame if we both went off in our own directions and you didn't know what a beautiful thing had happened. And even though it didn't work out, that's all right. I'm . . . I'm glad that it happened. You've touched me. And I wanted you to know."

"Whew." Bob let out his breath. "I didn't expect that."

John smiled. "I don't think you were ever aware of it."

"Oh, I was aware of it. I had heard some things. I just . . ." he trailed off.

"You heard things from other people but never from me." John chuckled. "I just hope you have some good feelings about what happened."

"I do."

The moon came out from behind its cloak of clouds,

making Bob look up momentarily to see why it had suddenly become brighter.

"So do I. I felt good with you, Bob. I . . . I hope I didn't upset you by telling you all that."

"No, no. Of course not." Then he added almost as an afterthought, "Really."

"Must be all this moonlight. Does strange things to people," John smiled and kissed his friend on the cheek.

Bob stood still and watched him slip into the driver's seat. The door slammed. The engine started. Two smiling eyes stared up at him, "Bye."

The car began to move. Bob smiled back weakly and waved a hand. He stood in the gravel parking lot, a solitary figure with moonlight in his hair.

"Good-bye, John. I love you, too," he said softly to himself.

John waved his hand, as he turned onto the Boulevard and headed south toward Coral Gables and home. The reflections of street lamps whizzed across the windshield. Something rare and uncommon had happened there that night and he felt exhilarated. His joy seemed to gather in the center of his chest and expanded until he thought that he wouldn't be able to contain it. At several points along the way, he allowed a chuckle to bubble out of his mouth. He didn't care if anyone saw him laughing alone in his car. It didn't matter to him one way or the other. The windows were down, allowing the wind to rush in and chill his face. The stereo speakers reverberated with the closing bass guitar line as Gloria Gaynor sang all about life. John hummed along, *I am, I am*.

He thought about the event that had just taken place, reviewing the scene, rearranging it, relishing it. Carlos came to mind, and he wished he could go and tell him, but it had been so long since they had confided in each other. Matthew was gone. Shy Matthew, who was concerned about the prospect of being on his own, was off in another city pioneering a new life for himself. Who could John tell about tonight, this wonderful night. He would have to wait until Monday when he could talk it out with Janet. Of course, he would tell Janet. She would understand. After all, they had known each other for years. They were good for one another.